HEADLESS

STORIES BY
BENJAMIN WEISSMAN

LITTLE HOUSE
ON THE BOWERY

Akashic Books
New York

HEADLESS

STORIES BY
BENJAMIN WEISSMAN

Akashic Books
New York

TABLE OF CONTENTS

1. BLOODTHIRSTY MAN

2. MARNIE

3. TIPS FROM THE SENSUAL MAN

4. TECHNICALLY DADLESS

BLOODTHIRSTY MAN

To Amy Gerstler, the exquisite,
and Murray Weissman, perfect father

In loving memory of Wendy Lewis Moore
and Gracia Weissman

Acknowledgments

Humongous thanks to brilliant soulful pals Thomas Bernhard, Bernard Cooper, Dennis Cooper, Trinie Dalton, Dana Duff, Sean Dungan, Matt Greene, David Humphrey, Tom Knechtel, Bill Komoski, Rachel Kushner, Paul McCarthy, Laura Owens, Hirsch Perlman, Lari Pittman, Lane Relyea, Thaddeus Strode, Gail Swanlund, Johnny Temple, Lynne Tillman, John Wentworth, and Zach Yates.

Published by Akashic Books
©2004 Benjamin Weissman

Drawings by BW
9 Honchos (detail), 1995, gouache on paper, 43" x 34"
Collection of Hirsch Perlman

ISBN: 1-888451-49-1
Library of Congress Control Number: 2003109537
Inside layout by Sohrab Habibion
All rights reserved
First printing
Printed in Canada

Some stories in *Headless* originally appeared in: *Another City* (anthology), *Bomb, Documents Sur L'Art, L.A. Weekly,* The Little Theatre of Tom Knechtel (exhibition catalogue), *More & Less 3 (Hallucination of Theory), Parkett, Purple, Santa Monica Review, Snowflake, Unnatural Disasters* (anthology), and *Western Humanities Review.*

Little House on the Bowery
c/o Akashic Books
PO Box 1456
New York, NY 10009
Akashic7@aol.com
www.akashicbooks.com

HITLER SKI STORY

Adolf Hitler was not known for his skiing ability. He was not comfortable on the hill. The incline frightened him. To be blunt, he was a terrible skier, a bundle of conflicting limbs and joints all colliding at the groin. The whooshing sound of speedy skiers made him jumpy. He did not take well to icicles forming on his manicured mustache. He resembled a walrus pup with narrow ice fangs, a look flattering on some gentlemen, but on his face not so at all. When asked, *if you could be any animal, what would it be?* as cold-blooded and smooth-skinned as he himself was, the walrus, or any sluggish lower mammal for that matter, was not on his list, even if he gave an amphibious impression of breathing through gills rather than nostrils and mouth. Yes, he was fond of the whiteness of the snow, just as Ahab was mesmerized by the whiteness of the whale, but he was a complainer; he whined about cold temperature, moaned about fatigued thighs, his lace-up boots pinched his flat bony feet, and to make matters worse, he had wobbly ankles. The T-bar and Poma-lift disturbed his balls. Hitler read *Moby Dick* in translation, a gift from Goebbels, in the privacy of his own prison cell, while he was writing *Mein Kampf.* The salad days. He never learned English, unlike today's ambitious multilingual Europeans. Like so many lonely men of that period, and many still today, he masturbated to the scene in Melville's novel where all the shipmates join hands in a bucket of whale sperm and squeeze the gooey coagulants and sing a brotherly tune of labor and soul. If only Leni Riefenstahl could've put such a sequence together in *Triumph of the Will.* But it probably would've disturbed the *mise-en-scene.* Hitler did not own his own pair of skis. In order to appear like the common man, a *volk*-skier, he rented. On a similar note, Hitler was eager to trade in his penis for something less drowsy, but organ transplants, or substitutions, in that area of the body were not foolproof, and, as history has proven, severing one's own penis and surgically grafting on a new and better one, a bigger, more charismatic jimmy, is frowned upon and remains an unsafe practice. Hitler's penis floated about his crotch like a hollow pinky. He wanted his cock to sway, a slab of meat that commands respect, that could be pounded against tables and the tops of people's heads, and if it were to be weighed on a postage scale would register *at the very least* four pounds. How could a man of modest physical stature, he often fretted in the bathroom mirror, convince the population of a master race, when he himself, and his faithful but never-to-be-fully-trusted assistants (a group of unsavory men, some tubby and slow, others skinny with pockmarked faces), were, in a sense, the furthest thing from a sight for sore eyes, or for that matter, a thing of beauty? Handsome they were not. Der Fuhrer & Company were specimens of ill health, poor diet, and cryptic exercise. He dreamt that boys would drop their knickers and salute him, not with a raised arm, but with their young erections—long rows of adorable poles all at 45-degree angles. Hitler could only snowplow. He fell often. He pouted. He'd lie in the

snow and curse. He'd try to stand up with his skis pointed
downhill only to fall again. He couldn't follow instruction.
Then along came Miss Braun, a great skier: bumps, downhill, GS, deep powder, and aerial jumps. The fraulein was a
hot dog. Yes, Eva was fearless, to a fault. It almost cost her
her life. After a day of flirty skiing with Olympic champions
Gunter, Heinz, and Klaus, Eva would catch up with Adolf on
the bunny hill. She'd stop abruptly and spray a blast of snow
all over him, and then giggle madly. Sometimes she'd throw
out a hip, knock him to the ground, and sing, "Dolfy on his
duffer." She was always trying to get a rise out of him, bless
her naïve heart. Unfortunately his response was always, "I'll
kill you." She'd cry. He'd kiss her on the nose, he'd say
meow, and as with most couples, the little hurt would disappear from the mind. Hitler painted a watercolor of a man
sawing off his own cock. The idea haunted him. Of course,
he threw the picture away. If you can't salute with it (the
veiny human wurst) or eat with it (like a shovel) or fight
with it (like a sword), what good is it for, huh? he wondered, wiggling lifeless all one's life, waiting for the kind-
ness of strangers to bring it happiness (don't hold your
breath); indeed, more often than not it was the sweaty oblig-
ing palm of one's own. Hitler painted snow scenes. Those he
kept. Some he gave away to friends. He painted a male figure licking an ice-cream cone. A ski instructor tried to teach
him stem Christy but Herr Hitler would catch an edge and
plant his poles like he was digging for oil. Hiding his true
feelings, he insisted he loved skiing. Politics and athletics
were a difficult combination but he forced the issue. Similar
to the certainty and assurance of a slow-moving tank he was
content with the stiff ungraceful snowplow. Why learn
something new if it's going to get you into trouble and make
you look foolish? During a lunch break Hitler drew a sloppy
swastika in the snow with his urine. Then he drew an
upside-down heart. Then he dropped his ski pants and

crossed them both out with a loose splatter of feces. The great outdoors, he thought. Traveling without the proper ointments was a serious problem. He wouldn't permit anyone to film him skiing. The only conceivable image was of the headman standing with his skis at his side, or on his shoulder, or exiting the chalet, striding toward, *never away*, from the camera. He had a flat uninspiring butt which he would've also liked to have traded in for something else, something more solid and global. He scratched his anus like a monkey infested with ticks. He'd smell his fingers and fall asleep. He dreamt he was caught in an avalanche, buried under 10 feet of snow. A St. Bernard came to his rescue. Hitler was fond of dogs. He preferred dachshunds. The large hound spoke German. It said, *Wiedersehen*. And then, for no apparent reason, it defecated on his face. And yet, and this is the amazing part of the dream, the heat from the feces prevented him from getting frostbite and saved his life. Another close call. Sure, it was only a dream, but wow, what a good one, and then of course you might ask, why so much shit? Interesting question. It was three in the morning. Maybe a shit facial, he thought, with its many organic properties, would cure him and his ministers of their dire complexions. He craved chocolate. So much for heading in the right direction. He nibbled away. A fudgy night. Yes, a bar of chocolate, always by the bed. He closed his eyes and thought, I hope someone remembers me like this.

BLOODTHIRSTY MAN

The day I am born brings injury and death to many people. My mom is a beautiful lady with a huge scar running down her back from a surgical procedure that almost killed her. A lonely flute whistles a sorrowful note. As a little boy I sleep on the floor in the kitchen with the oven on and open to keep warm while she has intimate moments with many strange men in the bedroom—at least 10 a week, sometimes 20 or 30 when she is not menstruating. Their laughter and screaming booms through the hanging bed sheet that serves as a partition so I practice punching and strangling my pillow to drown out the sounds of their sex. *Violence conquers all.* I write that in my journal.

When I turn 15, an age where I could be of some use, I am compelled to pick up a lead pipe and beat one of my mother's suitors in the head until he is bloody and without pulse. Even though the men are bigger than me—on another night I beat a second man as well—they are easy to destroy with their heads facing down, always on top of my mother's. Killing her customers is not something she appreciates me doing, but I do it nonetheless, spontaneously, and I clean up all the blood and brain matter with soapy water and many sponges. Three hours after midnight I roll the men into garbage bags and drag them with great effort to the town dump. Since the men never tell anyone where they are going when they visit us, we never have trouble with the police. I pull out a kitchen knife and stab my football until it is dead. One night I stab my mom. Slit her throat. She is plastered on cold sake. I'd like to say it was an accident, but that would be untrue. Everyone in our neighborhood knows my mom is a prostitute. I kill her before someone else does. It's better that her son be the one. Along with instructions on how to gouge a person's eyes out, the Bible recommends that we clean the feet of our loved ones with the hair on our head. I dig a three-foot hole in the ground of the public park where townies bury their pets and that is where my mom rests in peace, bless her worried gutted soul. I pack up a knapsack with a plunger, hammer, pipe, hose, razors, wooden sandals, and a pith helmet, anything hard and sharp that can be used as a weapon. In the middle of the night I walk 10 miles to a new neighborhood, sleep under a bridge in a cardboard box.

Every day I steal things and get in fistfights. I meet a lot of people this way. I join a gang called the Teddies and quickly become the head dude by kicking everyone's ass. By 21 I am protecting and selling girls and being a stone cold cool guy with shades and a leather jacket, with the nickname of Noodles because I only eat ramen. One day I get jumped by 10 guys and have to lay low, drink sake, soak in a bubble bath, and heal my banged-up bones. A week later I'm having sex with one of my lady friends in the bubble bath and this guy walks in and tries to cut me with a rolling pizza cutter. Trombones blaring, swooshy cymbals crashing. I yell, hey dude, get the fuck out of here, who are you, but he keeps on swinging his arms, yelling, so I get out of the tub naked, with the exception of my underwear, and land a single roundhouse kick to his sweaty crooked face. I take the pizza cutter out of his hand and press a big snowflake pattern across his smooth back. Thin lines of bright red blood seep out of his skin like angel hair neon.

This particular incident lands me in jail, the first and only time in my life. I'm put in a cell with a man who never speaks: I call him Silent Man. We become friends by not looking at or speaking to each other. I enjoy our quiet times together. In jail I am reunited with many old enemies in a cell opposite mine. They start mouthing off so I say, are you my bitch, come paint my toenails you little cunt dog. They yell back that I am the cunt and I belong in a cunt kennel, so I spit a 10-foot lougie right onto the bars of their cell—a mucousy spit blob that dangles from the metal and reflects light as if it were a string of crystal—which flames their fury and only makes me happy inside, at peace with the world. The jailer gives me a green toothbrush for general hygiene which I melt down one end of with many matches, stick a razor blade into the softened end, wrap some wire around it to keep sturdy: Presto, I'm ready to cut someone in the face, which I do at the urinal the day before my release date when some guy gets aggressive with me for taking too long to pee.

When I get out of jail the world seems different. Girls in bell-bottoms. Go-go boots. Incense burning. Everyone wearing long hair. Pink sunglasses. In 24 hours I become a mod hip cat and return to my usual antics. I steal a leather jacket and walk straight to a bathhouse. The girl puts too much soap in the water. Bubbles hit the ceiling. We have sex with our underwear on. Both of us. Super kinky. That's how I like to do it now. Don't ask why.

So we're wrestling in the bubble bath, splashing and going crazy, when all of a sudden this guy somehow sneaks into the room and starts watching us. I say what the hell fucker, I'm real mad and I'm going to get so much angrier you won't believe it. He bows his head. It's Silent Man from prison, so instead of killing him, I towel off, we say hello, shake hands, and I ask the girl in soapy panties, a student at the university, to read a book for a while, which she does without complaint. After his release from jail, Silent Man tells me, he suspected his wife of being disloyal so he flew into a jealous rage and slashed her in the face. Turns out Silent Man was wrong and he feels very badly right now. I pat him softly on the back. The gesture ignites further grief. He begins to cry. I get dressed and look out the window. Never console a weeping man with a gentle hand. Emotions explode through the tear duct.

Outside I see five guys ready to fight. Silent Man wipes away his tears, blows his nose louder than a fog horn, and says no way dude, no fighting for me, I run a noodle house, come visit. I say no sweat buddy and step outside. This big gorilla asks me for a cigarette. I pull out my pack, shake a butt loose, and offer it up. He grabs one and jams it into his mouth. I spark a flame from my lighter and hold it out for him. Just as he takes that first puff, I drill him in the jaw with an upper cut. Down he goes. That's called a cigarette punch, works every time. Then I kick all their asses. So much fun. After the fight these guys, they are so crazy, they want to buy me drinks. I say okay dudes. So we go drinking and become good pals. We form our own gang with me as the leader. We call ourselves The Punks. We smoke a lot of cigarettes. Every night I get myself a girl. I am a cool bachelor.

One night I meet a girl who wears three pairs of Day-Glo panties. We wrestle in a bubble bath. Maybe we have sex. Hard to tell. I'm thinking yes. I feel her muscle around me but it might just be her thighs. She lies on her back and prods my BVDs with her bare feet. When will the eel return to the pink cave? For a split second I am happier than I've ever been in my life. Of course all of this belongs in my journal. Then she pulls a knife on me. From across the street a twangy banjo is plucked. She's a country girl. She says I raped her once and sold her to a brothel. Hey, no way girl, I say, not me. I throw my clothes on and she chases me to an abandoned warehouse and calls me a bastard-prick. We fight off and on all day. Harmonica music pours through the room. Real saucy. We make up. She asks about my childhood, my mom. I think, no mind games for me, chick. I mash my mouth onto her lips. A big make-out session ensues. A brassy trashy tenor sax curls down from the rafters.

An older guy appears out of nowhere and says he wants to join my gang. I say why not, lug-head. Every night I take a bubble bath and then go out and eat a steamy bowl of ramen. An older established gang called the 4-H Club shows up. This guy with a Fu Manchu wants to fight me. Don't make me laugh, I say, while sipping the cloudy dregs of my miso broth. I reach down with my right hand and remove the wooden sandal from my left foot and smash the goon in the face. Both our gangs get into a big brawl to the accompaniment of bongos in a three-two beat. A kid on a skateboard films us while a little girl pulls him along by a string.

This is the beginning of a big turf war. I want to drink beer and bust up some places so that's what we do and get real bloody fighting these new conservative 4-H guys in business suits, who are slow and fat and become humiliated super easily. We run and fight them some more under the same bridge I used to call home as a boy, which brought back many bad memories. A single deep note from a cello. A lone raven flies overhead and squawks. I kick one guy in the head and his face rips right off its hinges, like he was wearing a plastic mask. The 4-H guys ask us if we've seen the Punks. I say no stupid fuckers, we *are* the Punks, now fuck off and urinate in your pants.

Silent Man from noodle house materializes out of thin air and asks my gang to return to his place for sake. We drink for a while but then the 4-H guys raid the place with guns.

I'm shot in my left arm, my leg, and stomach. My crew carries me home. I might die. A doctor dresses my wounds, pulls out a giant needle for a blood transfusion. My girlfriend laughs and says she's Type O, like me, the universal blood type. During my recovery I fear the 4-H Club will try to kill me but instead Sir Big Ears, the head 4-H dude, comes peacefully and asks me and my gang to join his silly posse. He says that everyone in town wants me dead and without his protection I'm doomed. Sir Big Ears worships me because he likes the way I fight. I watch his eyes drift across the room like he's concentrating on floating dust particles while I think about his crappy proposal. I remind him of what he was like when he was a young street fighter. I tell Sir Big Ears, no way man; I don't belong to no one. I call my own shots. I give him the hang loose sign, laugh wild, then double over in pain. Noodles, he says, you are a stupid daredevil. You'll be rubbed out five minutes after I leave the building. The Ambassadors want you dead and they control everything. I say okay I'll join your gang, whatever. We do a smooth soulman handshake, bang knuckles.

I just like to fight and take baths with girls and fuck in my underwear. I laugh and then black out from the searing pain of my injuries. While I am unconscious Sir Big Ears continues to admire me and reminisce more about his youth. Down the street two choirboys sing in falsetto. They emphasize the words *killing* and *murder* with a trilling vibrato that displays an innate affinity to swing. Giving each word its due, their winged phrasing banishes sentimentality. Sir Big Ears has the gray skin tone of an elephant, with a huge flattened nose. His ears are purple-red, like eggplant.

When I'm well enough to walk I visit 4-H Club. Sir Big Ears performs the initiation rite to induct me and my boys into their dowdy gang. They use two carp as part of the ritual. Both fish lying down on a white platter, back to back. Not working together. Lonely, sad, weak. Both fish go hungry. Maybe kill each other. He flips the carp over. Fish, belly to belly, work together, eat well. Live longer. Now I'm in.

Lame ceremony. I do what I want.

Next day I'm gambling with lots of big bills fluttering from the sky like autumn leaves. Girls yelling and giggling everywhere. I have more sex in my underwear. One girl comes in and slowly takes off my cool shades. She says, don't I know you? Oh shit man, my old girlfriend, Carla Balz. I accidentally insult her by calling her a bitch and a whore. She flies into a jealous rage and calls me a faggot bastard. She pulls out a knife and cuts my new triple-panty girlfriend in the face. Then she says sorry for the disturbance and leaves. Not cool. When I get home I pull the sheets down to get into bed—am I a sleepy man, or what?—and there she is, with her knife, lying naked under the covers, the blade between her teeth like a Ninja. Very cool. My room, extremely messy. She calls me a slob. Comments like that don't really bother me. She says I have to pay to fuck her this time. No way, honey. She cuddles up with the knife and pretends to snore.

I'm feeling kind of antsy. I go for a ride on the subway train and contemplate my life. Every day another gang tries to get a foothold. I open my journal and write, *new guys talk big*. A lonely cowboy sits across from me plucking a burpy bass guitar, singing about life on the plains. The toes of his pointy boots curl up like bent spoons.

Back at headquarters me and the boys relax, get drunk, and cruise around. We see the Ambassadors hogging the street with their expensive clothes and big limos, so we ram our car into their crowd, honk the horn, and get ready to fight. Their leader, Kimono Joe from the old country, comes waddling up in a black silk robe and says I should show some respect. That's my cue to show him how fragrant my underwear is in its bubbly sex state and then kick some ass.

Word travels back to 4-H that we, the Punks, are moronic

fuckers, and that we insulted the largest cheese in Asia. Leader of 4-H cuts off his pinkie finger to apologize for my bad behavior. Now we're in really deep shit. I retreat into laughter. More thugs will be coming to mess with us. An airplane lands. A pile of mobsters cram into five limos. Through the rear window of each limo, on the shelf where a box of Kleenex usually sits, there are bunches of dried chili peppers that symbolize angry hot brain. Not a good sign. Fancy shoes clacking on the sidewalk. On the train tracks my gang attacks them with pipes and baseball bats. We run through a tittie bar. One of my boys is stabbed, bleeds to death. That night we get drunk and honor our lost comrade with silence and sorrow and then many lewd jokes. Question: How do you stop a dog from humping your leg? Answer: Suck his dick. I look at a photo of my dead friend. Light cigarette. Burn sad pictures. Pour whiskey on flame. Poof, just like lighter fluid. Man, this feels like the end. One of my boys wants to quit. No more fighting. Buddy don't, I say. Wind blows in through a window. Flame goes out. A squeaky violin worms its way down the stairwell. Buddy leaves. Takes his share of the money. More hard feelings. I almost kick him in the face but I don't.

Ambassadors and 4-H waiting outside, chase buddy down, run him over with their limo. Blood pours out of his head like syrup. I am so angry now. Totally out of control. You ain't seen nothing. Another big fight at bathhouse. I pin a guy down on the ground with a picnic bench and choke him like helpless insect. Silence. Kimono Joe from Ambassadors lights a fat cigar. Load of guys in a huge hurry. Fifteen limo doors slam rapid. Sir Big Ears and Kimono both say surrender Noodles. My gang, very scared, almost crying. We must apologize quickly. Someone cut off a finger. Show Sir Big Ears that one of us has no finger like him and everything will be back to normal. Shiny pulls out a knife and says he'll do it but he just sits there trembling with the blade resting against his skin. He hands the knife to Mushroom Head and asks him to do it. He says okay but then he gets the shakes and bursts out sobbing. Everyone too big a baby. So I cut off my finger, no sweat. Pinkie gone. I walk outside with my boys trailing me and show both bosses missing finger, bloody hand, but they don't care now. Not good enough. Too late. They beat the crap out of us. Carla appears, tries to intervene, screams no, falls to ground. Now she's super bloody. Big knife wound. Silence. I have weird flashback about everything I've ever eaten: leeks, tuna, rice cakes from boyhood, squishy tofu, and, as an adult, every style of ramen. No booze, just solid foods. Then I pull out my knife and go berserk. Fight 20 guys. I cut one guy in the jugular and blood gushes out of his neck like geyser. Everything happening in slow motion. I get shot many times in the torso. A pale milky voice begins to sing as a flurry of spindly notes is tapped out on an antique harpsichord. My knife . . . it is far away from me. The Ambassadors pile into their limos. The leader gives my bloody body another long look, shakes his head, and then rolls up his window. The limos drive off. My journal blows away page by page.

I close my eyes, stop breathing, die, and immediately drift off the ground in a translucent vapor. A dog approaches my vacated body and marks my shell with a yellow pee squirt. My throat is parched, my stomach in knots. Once again all I can think about is food but the only thing I see on the street are little animal droppings, so I swoop down and chew them up as quickly as possible. Greasy and full of ash. I want to write *terror is the facilitator* but my journal is gone, so I write it in mud with a stick. Hovering against the side wall of HQ I see two older men wading through a muddy pit. They are shirtless, their hair long and wavy, their bellies ballooning out as if pregnant, their throats no thicker than needles with tiny blue flames coming out of their mouths. If they were strong enough I'm sure they'd fight me for one of these droppings, but they don't. It is important to realize how much excrement there is in the world and how good it tastes.

OF TWO MINDS

When the doorbell rings the boy sits in his room and grows short of breath. Ding-dong was what I heard while huff and puff emanated from my diaphragm. His mom yells *coming*, and five seconds later answers the door. My guardian screamed, *soon I will be there*, and a few heartbeats after that pulled open a wooden panel that swings on hinges. The boy is 15 years old. I was three years into puberty. The invasion is underway. The act of conquering and pillaging was upon me. His language is inadequate. My use of symbols—whether thought, written, or spoken—forever missed the boat. Paranoid: two voices in his head, simultaneously, fighting to be heard. I've had delusions of persecution and it should also be known that I nursed an exaggerated sense of my own importance. One voice is distant, observational, policelike, as if it were narrating all physical and cognitive action. The other was intimate, subjective, which is another way of saying, I'm all about double-talk. First he sees himself behaving in the present moment. Then I found myself blathering on about something I'd just done. Each sentence, *a shadow of its former self*, as they say. There's a reason he does this: the young lad suffers. I was a schizophrenic. He remains one. Many untrue things were said about me. He doesn't see himself as a person in the world, but rather a hapless character doing things in a story. I was never among thee. Please note that everything told herewith is true with the exception of the crime. No one prepared me for the psych ward. He is *an unreliable narrator*, as they say. I crawled through thick underbrush to slay the Gorgon. Constance, a lady he does not like, is here to visit his mom. A woman, whose name in Latin means faithful, stormed the homestead in search of my progenitor. This so-called friend of the family treats the lad like he's a moron. Whenever I was in the presence of the big lady I did something dumb and she made sure I was aware of my idiocy. At some point the boy is expected to make an appearance, to say hello. I, the one and only son, had two minutes to step out to the foyer and salute the Governorness of Creepville. Constance is sexually confusing to the young man. Because of my age and lack of experience in the world I had trouble appreciating a giant woman with a deep voice and a crew cut. Since he remains in his room, frozen stiff on his bed, it is only a matter of time before Constance and his mom barge in and force an encounter. Unwilling to budge, welded to my beloved mattress, the old grandfather clock ticked and tocked in anticipation of the aggressive, uninvited guests, who made it their business to fling open doors and demand conversation. He needs a hiding place. A secret spot was what I so dearly craved. The boy thinks of sequestering himself under his bed or squeezing into the closet. An idea bubble suggested I crawl beneath my sleeping quarters or flatten my body into the tiny room where ghosts have been known to lurk. He considers making himself invisible. I weighed the possibilities of becoming unseeable to the naked eye. The master of subterfuge walks into the bathroom and lays down on his

back in the bone-dry tub. I tiptoed into the water closet and
assumed a prone position in a vessel ideal for slitting one's
wrists. A bathtub that is never in use. Fortunate me never
encountered a pubic hair. The lights are off, the bathroom is
dark, a tiny streak of sun comes in through a narrow window above the mirror. There have been times in my life
when the rooms I've occupied have suddenly felt like caves.
Staring at the ceiling the boy prays that no one will see him.
With eyeballs directed upward I implored the Almighty
himself to let my physical presence go unnoticed. He is anti-
matter. I occupied the spirit world. The plan is for
Constance and his mom not to look in the bathroom, but if
they do perchance venture in to the land of gleaming tile—
please god no, make them not look in the direction of the bathtub. In the
event that they did happen upon hygiene headquarters and
their eyes drifted toward the coffin-shaped receptacle—
father of Jerusalem Slim, I beg thee, blind the whores. Outside a bird
chirps out a repetitive sequence that resembles Morse code.
I could hear a feathered vertebrate hoo-hooing a complex
message on a tree branch. His mother calls out. I was privy
to maternal bellows intended specifically for me. Oh
Benjamin! Son of Abraham. Come out come out wherever
you are. The wolf pack suggested I exit the fairy tale. Then
footsteps. I believe the audio went something like *klop klop
klop.* Two women stand in the boy's room. My crib con-
tained a pair of middle-aged broads who maintained upright
positions on feet. *Honey, where are you?* his mother asks. An
endearment was tossed my way followed by a request to
describe the location of my person. The boy holds his
breath. I sucked in a chestful of colorless, odorless gases,
mainly nitrogen (approximately 78 percent) and oxygen
(approximately 21 percent), with lesser amounts of argon,
carbon dioxide, neon, and helium. The women walk into the
bathroom, flip on the light switch, and look directly at the
boy in the tub. With the aid of a finger the two gals were

able to turn on an electrical device that enhanced their view of me in a setting that normally involves warm water and bubbles. There he is, as plain as day, or as unorthodox as a lobster on a leash. Me white, you, a large marine crustacean with a chain attached to your collar. Constance (her face flooded with wonder): *What pray tell are you doing in the bathtub?* The question, could you explain your behavior, was tossed my way via the bewildered bully. *Sweetheart, is something wrong?* the boy's mother worries aloud. An endearment was offered to me by my protector followed by an inquiring thought about my well-being. There are no soothing tugboats or cheerful rubber duckies available to console his anxiety. My state of uneasiness and distress about future uncertainties would not be quelled by the usual bathtub accoutrements that squeak and float. The boy remains motionless. I lay there, unmoving, paws glued to the outer edge of my thighs. An embarrassing moment for the boy. Mortification pulsated through my every pore. Lying down in a dry bathtub with all your clothes on is not a healthy act. As my shoes scuffed the porcelain I asked myself, *what is madness?* An oyster on the half-shell. A useless astronaut who no one wanted. His mother, Gracia, whose name and demeanor rhymes with Geisha, bows her head, looks away. The lady who brought me into the world, a woman of polite manner, steered her face in the direction of the sink. *Are you just going to continue lying there?* Constance asks as one of her eyes begins to close. The lady ogre wanted to know if I intended to spend the rest of my life in that position. Yes, he says. I offered an affirmative. *You are a strange and foolish child,* she says, *sick and in need of immediate attention. See a doctor who specializes in peculiar pipsqueaks,* she continued, *you're not playing with a full deck. Leave the boy alone,* his mother says, coming to the defense of her blood kin, *you're pissing me off.* I could swear she said, *Don't hassel the youngin I once called fetus or I'll rip out your lungs.* The kid arises. Just like that, I went from supine to upright. Passive resistance never works. I couldn't turn the other cheek. It's not a good idea to ridicule a boy whose favorite movie is *Bloodbath 12*. The last time I saw Constance she said my acne made her nauseous. He leaps at the horsy madame and begins to strangle her. With intent to choke, the galloping equine was advanced upon by yours truly. They fall to the tile floor. We crashed to earth, me on top of her. The mother, a trained actress, who's performed in numerous off-Broadway musicals, screams as the two bodies thump to the ground. With my lips and nose buried in blouse I heard a familiar high-pitched wail. Frau C closes her eyes and stops breathing. What I hoped would happen, did happen.

WICKED MAID CHURNING BUTTER (AFTER MR. ELKIN)

Even as a bear, I was unpopular. But I had no choice. I'd already made the change over, so I had to live with it. As a human, I was a disaster. No better or worse than the average fellow, you might say. No, say I was the worst. Please say it. And I thought being a bear would bring me luck, affection, and, most importantly, more food—perhaps, when by a river, a 10-pound salmon. What was once financially out of my reach at the supermarket would now be a claw's grab away. With some practice and a little inner fortitude I could do that. After my operation, I rumbled straight to the beautiful Sequoias of California, and the second I arrived I had sex with the biggest, hairiest bitch-bear the world has ever known—hear me out on this—she took my paw in her paw and jammed it between her legs. Once inside, she plunged it around like a wicked maid churning butter. Yes, my arm ached, but oh . . . and after it was over, after we kissed and banged noses, I gingerly pulled my arm out of her crotch and lifted it into the air to see dripping from my sopping limb a glistening blur of uterine juices. Then, of course, we did

other things, things only a heart should know. I'm not bashful, I'm a bear; I always will be. My hearing's improved. I
have not changed my name, I am forever Benjy, remember
me? the stupid lonely jerk—sad and smelly, but at least I
fucked a bear, what have you done?

MONKEY MAN KILLER

High anxiety sweeps through the hamlet of Frost Heave after the Monkey Man killer claims another victim, this time a postman, who was found impaled on one of his ski poles, mail satchel strapped to his back, no letter disturbed, three claw marks streaked across his frightened frozen face. A modest pile of cash, not enough to really change one's life, but a decent amount to make days and nights pass with greater ease, is being offered by the police to the citizen who supplies info leading to capture.

I was alone, reading the newspaper on the green tongue, our L-shaped sectional that has absorbed many years of coffee, whiskey, mango purée, lima bean mash, drool, dog ass, kimchee, a sampling of some of the best music ever recorded, leaky ballpoint pens, and a porcupine quill. My roommate, Dan, appeared out of nowhere. First no sign of life, and then, abracadabra, twitchy itchy Dan, dressed head to toe in black Carhartt, eyes blackened with baseball makeup, but no league games scheduled in winter with snow covering the ground like thick cake frosting.

Fleeing the notorious Monkey Man killer who swung from a vine above the Fountain of the Bashful Explorer, a bride and her sisters plus one aunt ran with flowers in their hair down a steep flight of stairs toward the foyer. The groom, trailing his future wife by only a few steps, suffered greatly for his slower feet by tripping on his unusually long coat-tails and tumbling down a hundred stairs, striking his head numerous times. Similar sadness occurred when a Frost Heave baker, fearing attack, jumped to his death from the roof of his bakery. Lonely, yeasty dough rose without the powerful kneading hands of its maker as police detectives scoured the white, flour-filled area for clues.

Grieving doesn't come naturally to me. Maybe if I comforted the baker's shy daughter at the funeral, who was crying and in need of comfort, she'd have sex with me on the floor of the bakery. She'd lift up her skirt and bounce on top of me, growl and cuss, choke a little death into me with her bare hands. Maybe that would relieve her sadness. That was what I hoped for. Question: Who will make the buttermilk donuts now that the baker is gone?

Groups of frustrated men are taking to the streets waving sticks, scissors, swords, tridents, and scimitars. Hoping to entice MMK, who might very well be an alien from a planet that sneaks glances at earth, the vigilantes carried perfectly ripe bananas with a faint streak of green on the skin as bait.

A confident chef turned his back on the flame and multitasked. I grilled onions but I was not physically in the kitchen.

"What are you cooking?" Dan asked. "What are you doing with the onions?"

"Potatoes Lyonnaise," I said.

Since Dan and I worked different shifts at the same restaurant we rarely inhabited the same room at the same time, but today we did, and it surprised me how nervous he behaved. I successfully calmed him down with a discussion about caramelizing onions, how important it is to allow them time to break down, to be patient and not incessantly stir or flip the translucent fellas which look like wiggly worms when tripping on acid, to give them their own private time with the heated oil, to brown in a skillet without distraction, otherwise the eater will not experience the remarkable transformation from harsh, tear-inducing bulb to silky sweet vegetable candy.

"Caramelization proclamation," we said in unison, but this time we did not tap knuckles like we usually do when we see eye to eye.

I took my dog Leslie, who hobbled gracefully on three legs, born without the fourth, out for a walk. Her fur is the color of wet sand. She liked the feel of fresh snow on her paws. When we approached the Fountain of Mystical Formulations I realized I was walking in my sleep, that I had not officially woken up from the previous night's slumber. Or maybe I did and Dan sprinkled snooze dust into my hair. "Sleepwalker, take yourself home now," I said to myself, but I just stood there, teetering left foot, right foot. Once the perverse aroma of night blooming jasmine entered my nostrils my eyes fluttered open. Awake, I bore witness to a little gentleman who performed an unusual act, but my frozen blood and trembling arms caused temporary inaction on my part, and a mild form of blindness. Was the little gentleman Dan?

The Monkey Man has three buttons on its chest. One allows it to become a monkey, the second gives it extra strength, the third makes it invisible. When he touches a locked door, the knob falls off and breaks.

Dan and I first got to know each other over the restaurant's bouillabaisse, and how it was originally brought by angels to the Three Marys when they were shipwrecked on the bleak shores of the Camargue. We lamented about our bouillabaisse and how much it sucked because frozen rock fish lacks the high gelatin content necessary for creating that slightly cloudy look, not to mention all the microscopic finny tidbits that make each slurp oceanic bliss.

Some citizens, believing that you can rob the Monkey Man killer of his powers, are standing by ready to throw water on his chest. The creature's motherboard heart, concealed beneath its thick black coat of hair, gets short-circuited by liquid. The police struggle with their homicidal instincts suggesting that we all shoot MMK on sight.

I punched my mechanic in the neck thinking he was Monkey Man. He fell to the snow, cried out for help. I felt very bad but he looked so much like the simian marauder when he rolled out from under my truck. So terribly hairy, wearing black greasy clothes.

Snowflakes fell gently from the sky, a day to chill on the green tongue; we watched *The Naked Chef* on the Food Network.

"Dude," I said, "did you know that a chef's hat is called a toque?"

"What do you mean?" Dan reached into his crotch, peered inside, scratched.

"I mean, that the classic chef's hat was invented by French stoners who were toking burly weed and they named their big hat the toque."

Without warning Dan lunged at me. I received minor abrasions. Fearing infection I walked through snow and visited my doctor who offered me an overly priced rabies shot, which I refused. I opted for the modest tetanus shot.

Some people say MMK is painted silver; others have stated that he dresses all in white and is covered with bandages like a mummy. Only his bulging eyes are visible. Sometimes he wears safety goggles. There are also Monkey Man copy cats who don monkey masks and take advantage of the "fearpsychosis" of citizens so they may scuffle and loot.

My doctor described the maniac's mind to me: MMK, he said, is probably suffering from frustrations. He continued to freely espouse that the sufferer takes on a role that allows him to exercise control over people who would otherwise treat him as a failure. No one wants to touch him.

Then there was the poor little girl who was beaten because residents said that the devilish soul of a Monkey Man had inverted her body. She appeared upside down, bouncing on her head.

The phone rang. I answered. A halting voice on the other end. Dan's Hungarian love interest. Her name was similar to *onion*, but without the consonants. Before I had a chance to communicate a warm greeting, Dan grabbed the phone from me, turned his back, and emited an "ooh ooh," then waited and laughed when he heard the caller make the same sound back, i.e., their not-so-secret monkey code. Dan's incisors come to fine points. My teeth are all rounded for softer foods: oatmeal, ice cream, and éclairs. His teeth are for removing bottle caps. He and his insect-eating girlfriend made a date to go bouldering. I've seen Oouioo pull down fir branches and snack on pine needles. Dan dropped the phone. Conversation done. He leapt into a handstand position, his hairy toes wiggling freely at eye level. He has drawn pictures of Mary and the Baby Jesus with those long-fingered feet.

"Save some potatoes for me, dude," he said, and then vanished in an unexplained manner. Suddenly there was a fire in the kitchen (oh no, the onions), followed by an explosion. I flew through the air and landed on my head, on the street. When I righted myself I found nothing broken or scratched.

A bicycle rolled by. A projectile slammed against our front door. The Sunday paper.

The headline mirrored my exact thoughts: HOW DO YOU KNOW WHEN TO BLOW THE WHISTLE?

PAJAMAS

When the Captain wakes up he can feel his brains moving around, hovering over his two eyes like a spacecraft, telling them to remain closed. The eyes obey. They are good soldiers. The day ahead will bring him, keeper of eyes and brain, much suffering. The rest of the Captain's body—feet, legs, arms, chest—refuses to fall into a pit of sorrow and regret, they follow the Captain's orders and continue down the path of pretend sleep. This goes on for hours.

The Captain is quiet, motionless. Once the eyes open there's no going back, he'll be in the world in the worst way, for another installment, but lying in bed, with eyes and body committed to an extended period of darkness, nothing terrible happens. He talks himself into believing that everything will be all right. Outside his window a cluster of mechanical birds imitate the sounds of pigeons, endlessly repeating the phrase, *who-who*. Earlier in the night, from 3 A.M. till dawn, before the machine birds, there was the chattering hobo lady, struggling with her identity song. She woozily sang, *who am I, who am I*, each time emphasizing the *who* or the I. Very often she leaves the Captain old baked goods from the health food store that are minutes from mold. In the middle of the day, when the Captain is far from home, he thinks about his bed and the powder-blue pillow, the only safe place on this entire planet. His room is next to a thorny, raspberry-colored bougainvillea. Other birds, birds far happier than the pigeons and their mechanical imitators, congregate in the big thorny bush, where chaos reigns in chirping dialogue. Several conversations going on at once. Bird social hour. What are the real birds telling each other that the fake birds don't understand? Are any of them worried about dying or is that just the Captain's continual fear? Do they think about anything besides the nest, a need for better twigs? Are there enough worms to go around? How impossible would it be for an old tired beak to snatch a piece of cotton? The Captain imagines being one of them, he conjures a horror story of marauding squirrels gorging on his eggs. His family is gone.

The Captain has a dim appreciation for what he is. As a person, he thinks, I have the ability to willfully limit my exposure to the outside world. He can flip a small toggle switch near his brain. Following a tiny bit of sound, a hum, an invisible wall of hard plastic, similar to the force-shield used by astronauts on old television shows, appears and seals off the area. In other words, self-control.

After eight hours of sleep the Captain can almost talk himself into believing that he'd never been born, that he was plagued only by his terrible imagination, that he'd never done anything wrong and he's not a worthless human being. He finds it difficult to convince himself that he's not just rotting away. Not a fast death, like all these birds that could die later today, but something slow and cruel.

With eyes still closed, the Captain pictures an unusual event from the previous day: A pigeon flew at his car and slammed into the windshield.

Just as he recalls the hollow feathery thump, his eyes open. He couldn't help it. He let his guard down. Vigilance, no longer his strong suit. And there it is, the shock of the banal day with all its secret threats. Time to repeat everything he's done before: boil water, make coffee. The doctor says no caffeine, so he does it for the smell, for the security, to pretend that the coast is clear. He shuffles outside to get the paper. He is not chained up. He is loose. Gravel feels sexy on the pads of his bare feet. If a neighbor were to suddenly materialize from an enclosure and address him with a *hello, what's up*, he would do his best to answer by saying the words, *nothing much*, and repeat the *what's up* question back to the neighbor because that is how people are greeting each other these days. He would also wave just in case his voice doesn't travel far enough to reach their ears. But no one physically appears from behind a wall or sliding glass door, there are no neighbors on the street. It is a few minutes prior to noon on a Thursday and all the residents are at work, therefore he goes unnoticed. Another miracle. Occasionally the Captain thinks he's speaking when he's dead silent. He has no idea what he sounds like. Like a garbage disposal or rushing water or a trash can rolling down the street? Once a booming voice, now barely above a whisper. Should he urinate in the middle of the street? He does have to pee and this does cross his mind. He remains civilized, returns inside.

The Captain inherited a lot of money from his parents when they died. He knew acquiring all that money would have a strange effect on him, and it has. This isn't a smooth transition. The happiness factor, or what there was of it, has definitely subsided.

Questions about getting out of his pajamas begin to pile up: Is it really a good idea? Is the Captain ready? What would he do once he took them off? Will a bath or shower be part of the day's festivities? Does he respond well to warm water and soap? Are there clean clothes to wear? Will this transition be as difficult as all the others? He got the idea of getting out of his pajamas from the newspaper. The headline read, *CIVILIANS, GET OUT OF PANAMA!*

He has become an outpatient in his own little ward, morgue, bedroom, bathroom, universe. Can he be trusted? Will he wander off? Is he truly ready for a change? Of bed sheets and life? Can he be trusted? Something unexpected could happen and that would disrupt the continuity. A door could swing open inviting in all forms of trouble.

The Captain's impulse to get out of pajamas was a positive sign. Just thinking about it seemed beyond anything he'd ever really considered since the inheritance went through, but it also made a certain kind of sense. He should be brave and just do it. But once out of his pajamas there are expectations that need to be met, his own, which he's not sure about, and the world's, that seem overwhelming and beyond his ability to cope. Is there a law against smelling bad? He really wants to know. The Captain looks down at his legs, the comforting black and brown plaid pajamas that haven't been washed since he purchased them; of course they need washing but they've also done fine without that indulgence. Aromas such as beef jerky, chocolate, and b.o. commingle in fabric.

An enormous fly enters the room even though all the windows are closed. It must be the same fly that's here every day but waits until midday to get things started. The fly couldn't be louder if it was playing the electric guitar. It travels through the room, taking stock. The fly hovers over the Captain as if he were a steaming pile, a compost heap. Eventually it lands on his big toe, and quickly figures out that he's not fecal matter per se, but just a strongly scented living organism with flaky skin. Once a fly hater from way back the Captain experiences a heart pang. He loves the fly. As far as the fly is concerned the feelings are mutual.

MORALITY PLAY (SIX HOURS IN LENGTH)

In tonight's show, contrary to our better judgement, we bring you an old-fashioned fable of *the unendurable man* known only as (raises his arm) . . . who wakes up one morning sick to his stomach; consequently, he vomits, looks in the mirror, and discovers a face as despicable and repellent as a moldy block of cheese, a smooth yet unshaven face which radiates a frightful bitterness—*malignant, demoralized, hysterical*—with narrow unappealing lips (pale and unkissable); *damn I'm ugly*, he says. In the classic American tradition of *following one's own drummer*, he sets out on a mission to destroy everything around him, starting with what's inside his apartment: the smashing of each light bulb and spotty window; the throwing of two wind-up alarm clocks, all 24 volumes of the Encyclopedia Britannica, wooden folding chairs, the framed family portrait, shoes, tomatoes, a honeydew melon, figs, which really opens up a *psychic can of worms;* the squashing of the goldfish; he lights the cat on fire, kicks the dog to death, shoots his daughter and son, strangles his wife, and heaves their newborn infant against the wall; *clutter*, he screams, *every person takes up so much room;* to calm his nerves he masturbates into a shotglass and downs his semen (*not as bad as one would think,* he thinks); after he disembowels the family one by one, an elaborate procedure well worth the effort, he breaks into an old lady's apartment, ties her up, defecates, and spoon-feeds her the stools; *my body's liberation,* he says, *is your midnight snack;* he masturbates a second time into the feces-covered face of the woman; laughter overtakes him and during this time he feels better than he's ever felt before; he wipes the tip of his genitalia with a surprisingly useful doily; *I'm finally doing what I want to do and I'm great at it;* he is exhilarated, close to tears, suddenly and wildly in love with life; *I'm the only person in the world able to do all this, I'm irreplaceable, I am great, I am who everyone wants to be;* he falls asleep and dreams he is on a vacation; he steps onto the terrace of a hotel to observe the ocean; he sees a marlin burst out of the water, fly over the sand, and dive into the hotel pool; *the ocean is so exciting,* he thinks, *so big, so majestic;* he shakes his head, *I like a fish with a dagger on its face;* the marlin jumps out of the pool and pierces a bikini-clad gentleman in the stomach; the unfortunate man and fish fall to the ground; he is happy as he watches blood gush out of the man; he wakes up, masturbates a third time, a record for the day, and sets the entire neighborhood on fire with gasoline and matches; *the world is passive,* he says as smoke rises all around him, *I am the active one, the spring rain of contempt, a swift morose icon, my gift is misguided love, I'm the only person who's truly supposed to be here.*

MARNIE

CLARE

Clare, who had recently customized her name to Clear, asked me if I'd be willing to get her pregnant, if I would have sex with her sometime soon, not just j.o. in a beaker and hand it over, but go somewhere romantic, and be a playful, studly friend, and fuck her so she could have a kid that looked half like me. I was on an informal honeymoon in New York City with my wife Heather Yellopey. Miss Yellopey is an architect. She is painfully beautiful with bright blond hair, big curious eyes, and lips thick enough to climb on. At night when she pulls down her black panties and exposes her astonishing buttocks and declares in a mock baby-girl voice that she's been bad and is ready for her spanking, I leap into action. *Ooh, my cheeks are aflame,* she has said on more than one occasion after her haunches have been walloped. The abovementioned Clare was an old friend from high school. We had sex a couple times by accident. Drunken staring matches, naked grab ass, someone's face buried in the other person's planetarium, mushy humping, out of sync—nothing dynamic. It always felt like what I imagined incest would be like. The familiarity was disturbing. We were pals. Our complexions were identical. Freckles everywhere. We even had them on our privates. Her ass was spotted. My dick. There you have it, inside and out.

Adjusting your name a little bit to suit your truest incarnation didn't necessarily seem like an overt sign of a deteriorating brain. The day after high school graduation Clare was on a plane to New York, escaping her oppressive, super-strict parents. She went from country bumpkin to a rock star's sex slave in a matter of weeks. The junkie bass player of the Dimples introduced her to sex with rope, toys, and knives. We stayed in contact writing letters, the occasional phone call. When I got a postcard from her signing off as *Clear* I assumed she was just doing some female version of *peace, later, out.* I didn't realize she meant Clear, like a glass of water; free from clouds, mist, or haze, i.e., *this is who I am now.* Since I don't have a middle name I used to give myself cool middles when I was in elementary school. I was fond of names of bullies in the neighborhood. I was Shane until Rocko pounded him into a fence like he was trying to tenderize him, and then I was Rocko, the badass greaser who threatened everything in his path. My parents told me that Jews didn't have middle names. I finally settle on T-Bone.

Clare's name change wasn't as disturbing as her insemination proposal. Heather, or Miss Yellopey as I sometimes like to call her, and I met Clare for a lunchtime breakfast at a Ukrainian restaurant. Nothing strange happened. The experience was normal except that the toilet in the men's room was not in good working order. After flushing I charged out of the bathroom like a hunted animal. Everyone in the restaurant knew that I'd paid a short visit to hell.

"Don't go in there," I said to a bearded stranger walking toward me.

"Why?"

"Because it's alive, and it's coming this way."

Clare and I hadn't seen each other in several years. She was still thin and muscly with bright orange hair. We threw our arms around each other for the big reunion. Then she turned to Heather.

"Hi, I'm Clear,"

"Hi Clear," Heather said, in observance of Clare's new name. They shook hands.

We all sat down at a table. Heather and I held giant menus in front our faces, big laminated shields. Clare knew what she wanted to order. I wasn't against her new name; I just couldn't bring myself to say it.

"Nice ring," Clare said. "Your wedding ring. Very nice,"

We both dropped our menus.

"Thank you," Heather said, genuinely touched by the compliment.

"How come you don't have a ring, sailor?" Clare asked.

"Because I have ugly fingers."

"What? No you don't!" Clare and Heather said in unison, and demanded proof.

Both beauticians spent 20 seconds extolling the virtues of my fingers (Heather inspecting my right hand, Clare doting on the left), how each digit was either gentle, masculine, or both, each with the proper amount of hair, wrinkles, et cetera. Fascinating stuff.

While the girls poked their way through delicate lentil salads with endive, goat cheese, and tomato, I lowered my jaw down to the table and swallowed my usual gargantuan portion of three over-easy eggs, home fries, kielbasa, sauerkraut pierogi with apple sauce and sour cream, toast, juice, and coffee. I wanted to show my appreciation for being alive by eating a lot.

We walked several heroic blocks through the big macho city, striding across the concrete, focused and determined, like the other speed-walkers, with a specific goal in mind, a bookstore. In Manhattan if you don't walk swiftly, aggressive pedestrians bump you from the left and right, and once you've fallen to the ground you are trampled underfoot, and robbed. Another secret to this East Coast streetwalking thing, *never doubt your path.* Plow straight ahead, do not falter. Once you hesitate you are on the ground, bleeding, a waffle print on your face. Clare, Heather, and I marched up Second Avenue. There was no attempt at conversation. I take that back. The girls spoke but I was oblivious to the content. I had the responsibility of protecting everybody. I concentrated on the ebb and flow of civilians. Clare led us to this gigantic used bookstore called The Strand that had an oniony mildew smell with a little dead body thrown in. I'd never seen so many people in a bookstore at the same time. Every aisle had multiple bodies in it. New Yorkers bought books more aggressively than desperate people in bread lines demanding a loaf. A pile of heavily clothed bodies entered The Strand, checking bags and backpacks, while an exiting dozen were lined up by the register throwing down big bills for armloads of books. Three minutes in, Clare hit me with the question.

"I have to ask you something inappropriate." She looked like she'd just peed on a Bible and wanted to do it again for the cameras. Her chin was tucked down and her eyes half rolled back. She smiled like a murderous clown.

"Really? What?"

"Never mind." We were standing between Art History and Holocaust Studies. "I'll talk to you about it later," she said. "On the phone. Maybe in a letter. Maybe never."

"Tell me now." *Hitler's Willing Executioners* was inches from my blue-ribbon fingers. "You can't build up to this and then say some other time."

"Yes I can." She liked that she had me.

I scanned the store for my beloved. A gloomy, disheveled-looking male employee crept through an aisle, pushing a cart of books. Miss Yellopey was out of ear- or eyeshot, hunting for books on gardening. I wanted to hear the inappropriate thing.

I know I'll get her exact wording wrong but it went something like this: *I'd like to have your child,* or, *I'd like to have a baby with you,* or, *I want to have your baby.* This was followed by another horrifyingly passionate I-dare-you stare. The delirious smile was gone. Clare was a girl with a sense of humor who never actually said funny things herself. She laughed a lot. At this moment she was as serious as a war monument.

"You're blushing," she said.

I felt my face. It did feel warm.

I looked around the store but I couldn't see anything; a little hysterical blindness in effect—all the books and shelves and people blurred into a brown speckled mass. Then she kissed me on the cheek. Charlie Sperm Bank and his adoring fans. A perverse wave of flattery poured over me. In an ideal world it would've been great to say, *How many kids do you want? Shouldn't be a problem. Meet me in the bathroom in five minutes.* A cartoon image of two oak barrels creaking from the weight of too much hollandaise flashed in my head.

"Think about it," she said. "You don't have to tell me now. Also, you don't have to worry about being the father or anything like that. I mean, you don't have to do anything else. I'll raise him myself."

"What?" I was losing it, fast. "I'm going to browse a little bit, okay?"

I wandered to the opposite end of the store, into the farthest corner. She'd already picked out a sex. She said *him.* Miss Yellopey, looking like a lemon tart, sat in a chair reading. The model citizen. I swallowed and then worried she could hear the swallow booming out of my throat. The man with something to hide.

Clare didn't ask me to be romantic and go to a hotel with champagne and flowers. Those were ideas generated by the good people at Terrible Imagination, Inc., otherwise known as my sick head, an evil organism that's all too eager to fill in the blanks, add lots of water and gory details. The second I heard Clare say, *your baby*, I was the reluctant star in a gigolo movie. Maybe Clare actually said, *beaker, test tube*, or *Petri dish*, and I didn't hear her because I always shut down the system when stricken with fear. Didn't I just get married? Call me deranged but I think having babies with my wife is a better idea. Making a child via masturbation sounds like trouble.

"Father, tell me about it. How was I conceived?"

"Well, son, I rented *Cocksmokers 3* and whacked for 30 minutes until the nastiest blowjob in human history came into view. I splashed down somewhere near the slo-mo, hair-pulling sequence."

Maybe I'd feel less terrible if she had discussed the proposal with Heather.

"Yo sista," Clare says in fantasy #2, late at night, behind the meat-packing plant. "Give me some of that sperm. I want a baby now." She and Heather are toe to toe, in rival gangs. It's a very tense situation. "I dream about babies every night. I needs one. I feel it here." She rubs her torso. "I want an infant to slurp milk from my puppies."

"Sorry girlfriend, no sperm-distribution program in my house," Heather says as she swivels her neck side to side doing the palsied chicken. "Try Brooklyn Cryobank. I hear their donors are put through a rigorous screening process. My husband's sperm, you hear me, bitch, my HUSBAND'S sperm will never parachute into your twat."

Clare had lots of boyfriends—the guy with the target tattooed on the back of his shaved head, for example, Corlis Whitepie—he'd make an excellent father. Clare was 39, newly divorced, a late-blooming recent graduate of Columbia, studying psychology—volunteering at Bellevue, curing the insane. I'm certain she'd be an inspired mother.

This is how I thought it through if you can call it that, privately, inside my soggy, lackadaisical head. I didn't want to have this conversation with anyone, not Clare, Heather, nobody. Except maybe the boys at my neighborhood bar.

"So, how was New York?"

"Not bad, a runway model cornered me in a bookstore and asked me to inseminate her."

"She used the word *inseminate*? Was she German?"

"Irish. Billions of freckles. Orange hair. Very hot. Has that ever happened to you?"

"Hell yes. Chicks are always demanding sperm, and not just for baby-making. All the women at Dean Witter wear little vials of it around their necks. They use it as a spirit conduit to communicate with Kurt Cobain and other dead hotties."

I couldn't bring myself to tell Clare no. I didn't have it in me to even ask for a little time to think about it. I didn't want to hurt her feelings. I wandered the aisles of The Strand and continued to fold in on myself. This had shitty soap opera written all over it.

When Heather tapped me on the elbow and asked if I was ready to leave I did my best to utter a nonchalant, Black Forest, *Ja.*

I don't want to hand over the goo to an old high school friend so that in 20 years my son will one day seek me out, weapon in hand, and annihilate my face. Maybe that's an appropriate scenario, something I deserve. In the hospital my son and I have a peaceful reunion, as he apologizes for partially maiming me.

"Hey, Pop, sorry to cut you up like that. I was pissed. Lost control. No hard feelings, right?"

"I can't really talk . . . too painful," I try to say. "All these bandages . . ."

My felony-craving offspring looks a little like Clare and I with tattoos, multiple piercings, a Fu Manchu growing near his mouth and a lot of scar tissue by the eyes. He's a bouncer at The Roxy, and he's taking acting lessons.

"It was good to meet you, son. Good luck with your life. I'm not pressing charges."

Clare, if you're reading this, sorry to take so long getting back to you, but I'm ready to answer. I've slept on it for five years. I cannot have children. Every time I close my eyes, my friendly little mind makes up another terrible story and frightens itself—sorry to not be the donor-gigolo-stud you had in mind. My sperm is best used for spraying on bellies, backbones, and foreheads, for rubbing on rag paper, for finger painting.

CENTIPEDE

The bride and I went to a hotel by the beach for traditional romance. We checked in at 2:30 P.M. and didn't leave until dinnertime. We had a boom box playing the sweetest Mississippi blues while we were flying all over the room like evil astronauts trying to repair that oh so out of reach godhead meltdown button, blasting on and off the bed, tearing each other apart like wolverines and then, a knock on the door. Porn freeze frame. So I say, Yeah, what is it, and a dead male voice comes back with two words, Turn down. I say, What? The cryptic utterance repeats, Turn down. But the music is low and it's, what, eight o'clock. I say, Turn down the music? and the voice says, Turn down the bed, would you like your bed turned down, sir? No, thank you. We continued fleshslap in vaporlock until the engines of love layed us down to rest, whereupon we staggered around the corner and ate fish at a place we later learned was a Ku Klux Klan restaurant. It was called Whitey's Sandy Catch. The workers, all in their early 20s, wore flowered uniforms. Lanterns, udders, sails, and oars dominated the walls. The men's bathroom was wallpapered with life-sized photographs of bikini models posed beside hooded Klansmen holding barbeque tongs and spotty aprons. The combination of sailing, seafood, and lynching was difficult to comprehend but we were starving and we didn't really put it all together until after we were gone. Anyway, following our waiter Hermann's suggestion, we started off with a shrimp cocktail. I had a stein of beer and my bride knocked back a shot of tequila—she's a roughneck, she didn't want to eat, just booze, and get back to the bronco pit for more lewd thrills. I got one suggestion for all you bachelors out there: Marry a nympho, you'll be set for life. We both had halibut, cauliflower, and mashed potatoes, with rice pudding for dessert. After a short stroll along the water, we returned to our room for more carnal activity. At some point we fell asleep. I dreamt about Cindy Crawford. My friends were irritated by her presence. Cindy was equally unhappy even though she told me she loved me. Suddenly the smoke alarm went off, not the one in my brain but a real one in the room, but there was no smoke anywhere. My bride leapt to her feet and turned on a light. High above our heads we noticed something crawling in and out of the smoke alarm. It looked like a colony of spiders, but it turned out to be one long and very nimble centipede. I rolled up a newspaper—I'm brave when striking something one-millionth my size—and as it traveled out of one hole and into another, I whacked it, whereupon both the outer shell of the alarm and the centipede flew across the bed and landed on the carpet. My bride called me her hero but she was also disturbed. We searched everywhere and could not find the corpse. The centipede was still alive. I was tired. Poison me, kill me, I don't care, I needed to know how Cindy really felt about me. So I fell back asleep. In the morning my bride told me to shake my clothes out carefully before putting them on. I did and sure enough the four-inch monster clung to an inside pant leg. I shook him out and scooped him into a coffee cup. I repeated the story to the Klanswomen at the desk who both wore matching flower-print dresses. One younger, sexy one wanted to go up and see the centipede, while the older fatter one pleaded with me to stop the story. I told her I couldn't stop the telling because I was Jewish, and as wanderers of the world we confront vermin daily and insist on making the most out of it.

THE FECALITY OF IT ALL

Reader beware, this is not a pee story in the true sense of Number One. It is without question a Two, but peeing does take place, and without the expulsion of urine none of this would be worth telling. What happened yesterday could only happen to me. The sad events narrated herein speak to the core of who I am. Why this is the case I do not know. By sharing this story with others I will not learn more about myself, but I do it anyway because that's all I really have: accidents and memories and then a little theatrical show-and-tell for a select audience with whom I can hold my head high in shame.

I started the morning like any other: staggered out of bed, shuffled down the hall, dog and cat in tow. George, the cat with black and white tuxedo paws, wanted out. He's small and has remained a kitten. Gina, the dog, craved breakfast. I filled the kettle with Arrowhead, turned on the gas flame, fed Gina lamb-rice pellets in warm water, and brewed coffee. Then I entered the bathroom, not to j.o., just poo. The smell of coffee triggers the *movement*. I have always been as regular as the sunrise. Thank you very much, but it's not a talent, it's a court order. I picked up a catalogue of children's toys (nephew's birthday approaching) and let loose a gargantuan log. I screamed as it came out. From the bedroom, my sleeping Bride asked if it was a boy or a girl? Both, I shouted back. Still clothed in T-shirt, pajamas, and white socks, I gulped some coffee, read the morning paper (the new Prime Minister of Israel was once a military assassin who dressed up as a woman and killed three members of the PLO). In one quick motion, the Bride is out of bed, in and out of the shower, driving across town to get her hair cut—all this without a sip of coffee or a single scrap of food. I hunker down in front of the TV and resume the arduous task of dubbing rented porn tapes (three a day, just the good parts). I title the tape, *Rhymes with Corn.* During each edit I drink deep from a 64 oz. Nalgene bottle of water. After 30 minutes I refill the jug and drink more. Dubbing porn dehydrates me. In 45 minutes I've drunk 128 oz. of fresh, mountain spring water. (Many a fool has been attacked in a bathroom after a predator, lying in wait, patiently observes his subject guzzling beer, usually at a neighborhood bar, pool hall, or bowling alley, it can happen anywhere—the bladder fills, the cheerful unsuspecting drinker stumbles into the men's room whistling dixie, faces the urinal, unzips trou; while the subject releases his full bladder, the perpetrator of pain strolls in and finds his vulnerable, stiff-legged victim, looking down or straight ahead, it doesn't matter, nothing in the world would make his face turn and look, unless he was under five-foot-eight. Short guys need to be on the defensive, it's a fulltime job. If the abovementioned thug called out the urinator's name, he'd continue to stare at the round rubber thing with holes in it that prevents splashing and encourages American males not to use drugs. During this protracted 60 seconds, the attacker, who never had it so easy, strikes the bladder-releaser on the back of the head, and out he goes.) Soon I must urinate. I go to the bathroom and find the aforementioned big poop from an hour earlier still in the pot. Not in its natural configuration, but roughed up by the previous flushing. I pee on top of it, and then flush. Here is where our story begins: The XXL doesn't go down. It chooses a different direction. It resists gravity and travels upward, toward heaven. As the water rises to the rim of the toilet I'm thinking the usual: This isn't possible, not here, not on this street, in this town. But yes, it will happen—your secret, morbid life erupts; the toilet overflows with your soft sculpture. The "mirror phase" and "potty period" and all the other psychological stages that you never quite made it through come to mind because you are not a mature person. Adult in age, not by action or thought. I was calm, enveloped in self-reflection as fecal water poured onto the tile floor. While murky water approached my feet, I hopped onto the counter, took off my socks, rolled up my blue-and-white–striped pajamas, and waited for it to end. A very familiar grape leaf floated by. Just a fragment. Everything up to this point could not have been avoided. Here I made my first mistake. I scooted off the counter, stepped barefoot into the mire, and flushed the toilet a second time (in all fairness to myself, the genius, the plunger was downstairs in my playpen, my office, I had been drawing pictures of it). Several more gallons of water flooded out into the bathroom, down the hall, and into the Bride's work cubicle. It was time to move into action: green light on rescue operation. A tornado of shit halts your melancholic, porno-dubbing life and slams it to the ground. You grab a bucket and a dry, aging sponge-mop that practically says, *Who me? I can't do anything,* and go at it. You start in the bathroom, where the tragedy began, and work your way out. After two useless minutes, the sponge peels off the frame of the mop so you grab the oldest, least attractive beach towels in the closet and commit them to biohazard. A 90-minute job which included a final rinse of Pine Sol. When the woman you refer to as "The Bride" returns, you are in the kitchen, in a room that has not been damaged, but you are so obsessed with cleaning, with turning around the malicious direction of your life, that you can't stop yourself. Just by rubbing you can make a stain vanish from the earth. That's a powerful act. The Bride looks even more beautiful than when she left, especially from the floor, which is where you are, on hands and knees, mouth open, a broken-off piece of sponge in one hand. You are fond of this hapless sponge. It pitched in. It did what it could and stayed with you to the end. Not many sponges would do that. You'd kiss it if you were alone with it.

"You got inspired to clean," the Bride says. "How nice of you."

"I wish I could take credit for such a noble gesture but I can't," you say, sounding strange. "That's not what happened."

"What happened?" she says, removing her leather jacket, dropping her beautiful black purse on the table.

"Something terrible happened," you say, and then you retell the story. A big shit, massive overflow, no plunger, a second flushing, water everywhere.

"Poor you," she says, "that's awful."

And then, like always, you go too far with your descriptions. "Yeah, I even saw the grape leaves I ate yesterday."

"Yuck," she says. "Now I'm going to barf."

Why would you tell her something like that? You look down and see another spot on the floor and rub it out. Then another. Soon the Bride, who frequently takes on the role of nurse with you, tries to lift the pitiful patient off the floor but he weighs too much. She tells him to stop cleaning.

"It's over," she says, and kneels down, kisses your sweaty forehead. She is infinitely kind. "I'm going to make myself a fruit drink, do you want some?"

"Can you smell it?" you ask.

She tilts her ballet-dancer face back, and sniffs. "Well . . ." she says, and closes her eyes for fine-tuning, "sort of."

You stand, a little light-headed (ah, the elephant rises). Suddenly there's nothing to do. The job's done but you won't let go of the sponge.

The Bride walks into the bathroom and lights a tiny pyramid of incense. You go down to your playpen in the basement thinking this would make a good story. In a way, you enjoyed the experience.

Sometimes you leave your laptop computer on all night and that's what you did last night. When you approach your desk, you see water everywhere, books, papers, and drawings soaked, and a smell even worse than your previous upstairs encounter. First you were ankle-deep in goop. Now you are under it, a thin layer of feces above you. You look up and see a big coffee-colored drip.

Say it: "I defecated on my computer."

You just clean and clean, that's what you were put on earth to do. You mess yourself, you wipe, you crawl around, and then you clean some more. You pick up all the sopping wet papers, smeared and stained, and throw them in the trash—don't even think about what you've ruined, just dump it all in the basket. Oh look, all your plunger drawings. You hang them out to dry on the clothesline, 30 of them, reeking and streaked with brown. Since you're one of the infirmed, it makes sense that you live and work in your pajamas. Now scamper upstairs like a nice boy and tell the pretty lady what else has happened. The whole process is second nature to you. You take all the dung-infested books outside and stand them upright with the pages fanned out. Maybe they'll dry without sticking to each other. But is it really possible to read Emily Dickinson when you know that every page has been simmering in your own excrement?

How do you get something like this repaired? If you send feces in the mail the government will prosecute you. It is indecent and against the law. Even though you're a person with a short fuse, none of this has caused a serious tantrum.

In fact you have not reacted. You're numb and at peace. Your breath is steady, and that terrible smell is fading, or so you'd like to believe.

O please, dear reader, drop that stone. Do not judge me, for I am an unfortunate person, a silly man, who doesn't know up from down. Open your heart, diaper me. Lay me down in my crib. Press a cold compress to my brow. Let me rest. My world has caved in and I am weary. If there's a lesson to be learned, maybe it's this: If you feel a giant Number Two coming on, flush it down in installments, not all at once; and if your plunger moonlights as a model for figure-drawing, make sure you acquire a second plunger that is young and full of appropriate suction. Humble is the man who is backed against the wall by his own bowel movement. Lest we need to be reminded, the rear end is the devil's public address system. It points in the opposite direction for a reason, to contradict all the good the face and eyes create, and it will always steer us into hell.

BABY HAIRS

Baby Hairs has terrible luck with women. He could use my help, but Wilhemina, the roadblock, said no. I wanted to set up Baby Hairs with Carla, but Wilhemina, Carla's friend, thought it wasn't a good idea. I thought it was, and I'm the premier matchmaker with a short list of miraculous successes to my credit, pairings that naysaying bystanders initially poo-poohed but eventually marveled at, which is why I thought but did not say to Wilhemina, *Back off, chick, get out of my way*, because I'm polite, calm, even-tempered, and I know what I'm doing. I'm a pro.

Wilhemina said she didn't think Baby Hairs would like Carla. Since I knew Baby Hairs better than anyone on the planet, and that includes members of my immediate family, I didn't think she had a leg to stand on, which is probably why she made this discouraging remark slouched in a chair, weary and wilted like an old banana peel. It wasn't that she hadn't thought about this unique pairing deeply. I'm sure she had. I just think she has a corrupt take on things that serves herself over Baby Hairs and Carla, which brings us to a key point.

A matchmaker must never think of himself, or herself, when embarking on the coupling of others. It's one of our basic commandments, along with Thou shall not needle, nor pry, pressure, police, nor make predictions, mediate dialogues, send gifts, chaperon, escort, salivate. Following in the footsteps of O.M., the Original Matchmaker, our methods must be covert, subtle, and yet, like the King of Kings, we must remain humble, modest; our heads bowed, never looking for standing ovations, even if we deserve them.

Why was Wilhemina disrupting my beautiful pairing? I threw coins and the I-Ching said, "Energetic progress in the good." Foolish me assumed that Wilhemina was a fellow matchmaker. Aren't we all, I sometimes ask myself. In other words, once we find love and happiness for our own body and brain, like food and shelter, isn't it our obligation to make said necessary items available to others? Even though she hadn't really thought about the situation as deeply as I— which is understandable since I'm the fellow who has seen bleak lives of solitary confinement featuring mismatched socks, infrequent bathing practices, and poor oral hygiene blossom into something approximating happiness. When love had the possibility of entering the lonely hermited life of Baby Hairs, she said *No,* and when I persisted she stuck with her answer, *No* again, only this time a bigger, more emphatic *No,* an angry *No* that featured bulging eyes and tense facial muscles that hinted at door-slamming, thick phone books heaved across rooms, fire extinguishers, restraining orders, and the like. That, needless to say, sent me into a tailspin. I had trouble with her edict, the final word from the top boss in a sealed-off room with thick bullet proof glass, a *no means no type of no,* which briefly turned me into an adolescent. So I said, *Who died and elected you bully queen? Show me the corpse and the death certificate of the previous tyrant, if you don't mind.*

And then I switched gears: *Charming Wilhemina,* I rehearsed privately to myself, *associate of the planet, comrade in arms, why are* we *fighting like this, struggling over the potential joy of our friends, risk-ing our own solid rapport as earthlings and love scholars?* She of course must have thought, *Why does my life have to by marred by the existence of you?* and that was my point, that she and I were unimportant players in this romantic equation about our special needy friends. In this way the matchmaker is more scientist than social worker. Don't disturb my lab work. My subject needs plenty of air, water, a room with a view, and loads of affection. He needs to be scratched on the back of the head, spoken to softly.

Then Wilhemina shocked me with two revealing admis-sions. One, she said that she was no longer friends with Carla; and two, that the commingling of Baby Hairs and Carla, her sudden ex-friend, would make her *uncomfortable.* These statements were made while seated in the same chair, her posture even more melted than previously mentioned. *Uncomfortable?* I thought. *Uncomfortable* like a stray eyelash jab-bing one's cornea or a paper cut or bunched-up underwear creating havoc with the genitals? *Uncomfortable in what way?* Hunched over my rolltop desk, I couldn't stop repeating the word *uncomfortable* because I couldn't stop thinking how much smaller than an atom that statement was when observed under my infuriated cerebral microscope. *Uncomfortable how?* Where do I gather the strength to respect such a tiny particle of utterance? What type of mechanical instrument should I use as a hearing device to comprehend this oral discharge? Where does earth supply its citizens with the fortitude nec-essary to cope with such foolishness, and challenge wrong-doers? I also thought, *Uncomfortable why, uncomfortable because you now resemble discarded objects frequently seen in dumpsters?* So badly I wanted to ask Wilhemina this, along with a theatri-cal, *Who the hell do you think you are?* which my mom said on a daily basis to windows and mirrors, as well as actual people like store clerks and waitresses. Since I have never said such a thing to someone's face before, I was at a loss as to how to deliver or perform my righteous question, which is why I kept it all to myself. I have cowardly genes. I shy away from confrontation. I actually fear real interaction and cross words. Just the thought makes me shake. Consequently, insults grow in my head like boulders of hemlock.

Wilhemina said she didn't think Baby Hairs would like ex-friend Carla, because ex-friend Carla is difficult and troubled, kind of a freak or lunatic, depression prone, that she can be a scary psycho at times or every second. And then I said—I addressed her as Lil' W, thinking maybe if I pretended that we were both truck drivers talking on CB radios I could get through this conversation without crashing head-on into another semi-tractor trailer—I said something to the effect of, Lil' W, that's music to Baby Hairs's ears. That's exactly what he craves, really and truly. He desires the mental-ward girl, the smart, cute, sexy fräulein with black hair blunt-cut in a 1920s Berlin style. Plus she has a cleft chin that makes her sort of masculine. Baby Hairs's last girlfriend, a person he met on his own, turned his car off while they were driving on the freeway and threw the keys out the window. He had to roll to a stop, guide the car to the shoulder with the steering wheel locked in place, climb the low concrete barrier, and retrieve the keys while oncoming traffic zoomed close and threatened manslaughter. Desperate maniac love, that's what he likes. Fighters.

When I informed Baby Hairs a few days later, at lunch, while he ate his high-protein cottage cheese scoop and hamburger patty with multiple squirts of catsup, that Wilhemina was running interference with my matchmaking, that she said, *No, no, no* about hot, sultry Carla, his first reaction was a simple, *Why*, and then he, child of Freud, asked the million-dollar questions: *Did Wilhemina say no because she craves sex with me? Is this not a classic case of displacement? Does the young lass want me all to herself?* This is one of many reasons why we love Baby Hairs and why we're working overtime to find him conjugal happiness and why he holds the Kraft-Ebing Chair in the Psycho-Sexual Dept. at Fontanel University. He is prone to insightful observations such as, "The ego which has discarded all ethical bonds feels itself at one with all the demands of the sexual impulse."

I was quick to say, *No, she does not want you all to herself,* before I really had a chance to mull over the intriguing possibility of Wilhemina, a lifelong dyke, breaking lesbo rank and lusting after the flat hairy ass of Baby Hairs. One year, 10 months, 14 days ago Wilhemina fell in love with The Angel, the greatest little femme our earth has ever known, and they are happy together, perhaps ecstatic is the appropriate term, which is why they recently acquired a talkative Mexican Parrot that repeats the phases *Shut up* and *Eat me* all day long. I also said *No* because I didn't think we should get sidetracked, and *No* because I didn't believe Wilhemina was thinking, *Must retain Baby Hairs as hetero side dish,* but I'd be lying if I said it didn't get me thinking in another direction: Maybe Wilhemina the Selfish, Wilhemina the Jealous, doesn't want to see Carla, her skinny, pale friend with the dented chin, win the prize.

This is a difficult predicament for someone like me, a person with a discrete halo over his head, pusher of all things fair and true, to see Wilhemina hogging an inordinate amount of life's pleasures for herself. Understandable if one were to see things from an adolescent's point of view, but still not right at all, something the Bible warns us about repeatedly in Deuteronomy, the fifth book of Moses, and Genesis 33 where Jacob conciliates Esau.

Am I good? Baby Hairs, the cryptic, asked during a moment of low self-esteem. We had just hiked to the top of a giant snowfield. It was late spring; the snow was granular and melty. We were playing chess on a tiny magnetic board. Each move had to be done carefully, the tips of our fingers functioning like tweezers. He was sad, his blood sugar low. He'd just lost his queen.

He reached down and scooped up a layer of snow and put it on his head, then rubbed it briskly into his scalp. Tiny fragments of snow remained in his thin wispy hairs. I removed a small camera from my backpack and took his picture. *Yes, you are good,* I said, *you are solid in every way.*

Solid like a stool? he asked, just as he smeared a cracker with liver pâté using his Swiss Army knife.

No, I said, *like a solid friend, a reliable horse, a monument.*

Baby Hairs is nothing like The Angel, who's perfect to the extreme with sparkling blue eyes that actually twinkle, as if lit by God. The Angel: soft, little, smelling like a bar of Ivory Soap, a sergeant of Sappho's army. Baby Hairs, the opposite, wanted to know how he seemed to people in the outside world. So I told him he was mad and loopy like Carla, this girl who he may never meet as long as he and she both shall live, that he's generous and brilliant, possibly even a catch (a fixer-upper might be more accurate), that he has more humor inside him than all the suffering comedians of the world; he's self-deprecating, doesn't talk about himself all the time (girls appreciate that), he dresses down, almost to the point of looking like a gentleman with no source of income. I've seen him wandering the streets in his bathrobe (girls do not appreciate that). Baby Hairs is tallish, six-foot-one, almost handsome, bordering on cute, with funny little hairs that poke straight up from his head like pin feathers on a newly hatched duck. Doesn't drink. He's macho, but not murderous. Comes from old Plymouth Rock (rip-off-the-indigenous-people) ancestry, born in D.C., his great-grandfather the governor of New Hampshire. On more than a dozen occasions, I've heard him say that his mother is a liar (i.e., hundreds of hours of therapy, 10 years twice a week, substantial emotional progress, yes, unfortunately continued pain and suffering). Baby Hairs, the spotted lamb with bitten off fingernails who was shipped off to boarding school as a young lad, was put on earth to love and be loved.

Also petted, scratched, kissed, teased. That much is certain.

I, a simple matchmaker, an agent with a magical gift of bringing people together, am trying to spread and smear love around as often as possible or whenever it seems appropriate, but I'm having trouble accomplishing this vital task. I could've signed off in resignation, saddened as an oppositional force tampers with my ability to work wonders, a rival, the anti-matchmaker, a shrew who will stop at nothing to keep her frisky ripe ex-friend away from my lopsided amigo, but I didn't. I violated certain trusts and statutes and side-stepped the human barrier and set up a clandestine meeting with Baby Hairs and Carla.

The three of us met at a diner owned by the brother of dead Mafioso John Gotti where the matzo ball soup has big pieces of chicken, carrot, and celery. Baby Hairs looked perfect. His dirty torn up Carhartts gave him working-class appeal, like he knew how to hammer nails. Carla wore a tight black T-shirt and nothing else. Correction: She wore pants and shoes, too, also black. She was ready to go undercover, to kill for love. When they shook hands, Baby Hairs revealed his perfectly broken smile. Carla leveled a deep smoldering gaze that seemed to suggest come hither, or come as your are, or come again? One eyebrow darted up and her upper lip curled slightly. If I said it was love at first sight I wouldn't be lying, though it could've easily been fear or repulsion. Those initial reactions are hard to gauge even for a professional like myself. You gather data and then you wait.

I took a deep breath and went to the bathroom and examined my own friendly face which seemed less green, more yellow. Why did I look like I was about to cry? My lips were parted. I was panting. Couldn't I breathe with my mouth closed? My ears were bright purple, new hairs sprouted at odd angles. My nose hairs were equally rude and Brillo-like.

The bathroom air vent was right next to our table. Carla was speaking. I overheard a mumble from her wishing I was gone—she called me *that creepy dude*—she said I took up too much air, that I smelled like a cheese product, that my interest in other people's lives was well-intentioned, but also intrusive, and kind of disturbing. She said I was kind of a loser. That's what she called me. She said it would be cool if our little matchmaker could disappear.

Not to worry. Been called one before. Losers are experts at being called losers. We know how to handle it. Special defense procedure in place.

Rule #1: Keep moving. Stay afloat. Mustn't injure self.

Rule #2: Stay cheerful. Smile through it. No tantrums. Breathe in love. Exhale hate.

Rule #3: Remain standing. Exit bathroom. Don't fall.

The uncomfortable silence, heavy as concrete, was poured across the table. I sat back down and looked at the two ingrates. Fine, have it your way, I thought, try and make it on your own. Without saints like me to set tables and jam napkins into your lap you'd be nowhere. You'd be eating out of troughs in a barn. *Oink* would be your primary verb and noun.

Okay farm animals, pick up the hot-seeded sesame roll that the waiter so graciously put in front of you. Try and butter it without clomping your hooves on the table. I must leave now, with my halo intact. The matchmaker has suffered a deep flesh wound. But he will survive and prevail and continue to service the community in ways no one will ever truly appreciate.

I gazed at Carla (she should really dye those unwanted facial hairs), tilted my head to the right, and smiled bold and brightly. I shared the same glowing expression with Baby Hairs. Make sure you use a condom, you fool. I closed my eyes dramatically, one one-thousand, two one-thousand, and let the full meaning of what I have just done for them sink in. And then I rose to my feet, turned on my heels, and walked home.

MARNIE

The first time I saw Marnie naked, she was lying on her back in an ambulance while two paramedics cut her yellow Burton shell off her torso. The zipper must've been caught on the fabric. The medical boys sliced her jacket and all the fleece underlayers right up the middle with a razor-sharp scissors as if she were a fish. They needed to get to her heart. Didn't we all? I stood a few feet from the sliding door of the ambulance in full ski gear, gawking, mouth open, the ultimate perv. Red ski patrolmen floated by, big white crosses on their backs. They nodded at me and turned away.

Marnie had huge amazing tits, bone white, with nipples as pink and ripe as guava pulp. It was the only time in my sex-crazed life that I stared at a naked girl and wanted to look away. We weren't together or anything, we were just pals, both obsessed with mountains and snow. We probably skied together 25 days a year, hiked, played softball in the summer with a gang of friends, drank beer, ran into each other at art openings and the occasional barbecue. She liked to throw parties. She had a backyard with lots of trees and places to sit. Maybe we were like brother and sister; at least she treated me like that. I was the advice guy, giving her counsel on books, and sexual strategy for boys she lusted after—and now I was freaking out on this rad view of her body, clothes peeled back, revealing the blinding treasure within.

No one told me to move. I wasn't Joe Sleezoid violating an injured woman's privacy. I was an indeterminate blob, a confused idiot watching his friend be manhandled by rescue guys. I was going to report all this shit back to her. Tell her that boys handsomer than Jonny Moseley—who knows what they actually looked like, I just knew that's what I was going to say—were rifling through her privates. She'd be creeped for life if she knew paunchy lumps were tinkering with her body while she was out.

Marnie was the best female athlete I'd ever known: strong, fearless, stubborn, smart, prickly, generous, humble, blah blah blah, freckly, and very flirty. She'd stand in the middle of the room in a tight thermal shirt, squeeze her boobs like a stripper, and say how much she loved them.

We met at Cal Arts, in the Grad. Program. One night after a screening of some Belgian art films (mainly Bas Jan Ader), a pack of us went out to Canter's for liquor and matzo ball soup. Marnie and I were both wearing the same Air Jordans. That was kind of it. We started talking about sports, a giant relief from art babble, and within an hour we had more than one ski trip planned. She made tons of badass sculptures and photographs. I painted sexually deprived robots with pitiful captions about tenderness. She wrote this corny love story she claimed she didn't show anyone but me about two inseparable cacti. She also took photographs of cacti and Photoshopped them into these lush sci-fi landscapes, and treated them like male/female dolls caught in a romance. I'd like to say that we were super suited for each other but we weren't. There was a stubborn brat in her that could stretch to infinity. When her behavior got particularly rank, she'd reach deep into the barrel and remind me of her only-child status, as though that was some kind of excuse for her acting like a tantrum-throwing freak. She was spoiled to the core via a pampering Pittsburgh granny. I was, and steadfastly remain, a morose gloomster, which is another way of saying: On occasion I irritated the crap out of her. But when I saw her lying there on her back all perfect like a netherworld deity my heart and whatever else went bonkers.

I expected her to wake up any second; all she needed was a little smelling salts or a few wet kisses applied by me. I've passed out a bunch of times and pretty much got off on the blurry disorientation. You think, who unplugged the projector? And the cool spacey thing is, something inside you yanked the plug. What you need when you disappear into the darkroom is a sober audience member to explain the missing minutes when you wake up. I was all set to get in her face about how rad her crash was as soon as her eyes fluttered open. Our tumbles were never embarrassing, they were spectacular Indy 500 car wrecks—loud football grunts, huge explosions of snow, multiple somersaults, skis and poles twirling in orbit, hat and goggles just part of the debris. But this fall of Marnie's wasn't like our usual crowd-pleasing highlights.

That morning we'd assembled our all-important turkey sandwiches with cheddar and avocado and four kinds of mustard that we meticulously prepared on the floor of our tiny motel room to the accompaniment of blasting Pantera, as if we had entered the World Heavy Metal Sandwich Competition, and, no surprise to us, we were heavy favorites to win. We wrapped them in foil and wrote *eat me* and *fucker* on them. The sandwiches hung from a tree in a plastic Vons bag, as per usual, but this time would never be eaten by us.

At 1 P.M., minutes before our feeding, we were on a short,

steep run that we pet-named Satan's Maw, a sexy funnel of snow, like a 400-foot tongue with super jagged rocks on both sides for teeth. A classic chute, something we'd skied a million times before, or at least twice. I skied down first—the scout, the hog. The snow was ice-rink slick on the sides, soft and carvey in the middle. It had rained for two solid days, and then it froze up, and snowed a few inches overnight. The conditions couldn't've been schizier. But when I got to the bottom, breathing hard, I was euphoric and psyched, blood pumping in delirium. Every little jump-turn, clean and sweet. The perfect run before lunch. Marnie traversed into the good snow, made a right turn, and inched her way over to the ice. I don't think she realized how slick it was. We hadn't really talked about it. What began as an innocuous little slip of the skis—just losing her footing at the top, tipping over onto her hip, no big deal, sliding for two seconds until a tree stump knocked her downhill ski off—became something much worse. She continued to slide, quickly accelerated, the other ski popped off, and from there she jetted straight into a huge pile of rocks, somersaulted over a small cliff, her body thrown back onto the snow where she torpedoed right past me, head first, a limp rag doll, until a small grove of baby fir trees stopped her on a dime. An ugly crash. The worst I'd ever seen in person. I skidded down to her. She was flat on her back, her legs twisted up at the base of a tree, one hand on her stomach, the other behind her ear. Her yellow shell was up over her head. I clicked out of my skis, jammed them into the snow, and kneeled beside her. I unzipped the top of her jacket. She was snoring. I stupidly thought, good, sleep is a good thing.

Then it hit me in a panic; this type of snooze is dangerous. Her eyes were open. One pupil appeared irregular, ruptured, blasted out. Her goggles, gloves, and hat were torn off her body. The temperature was in the low 20s. Her cheeks and the tip of her nose were pink. Frostbite not a problem, yet.

A chairlift was barely within earshot. I shrieked for help. I waved my arms and screamed, *Emergency, unconscious, ski patrol*, over and over again. Tourists on holiday, maybe they heard me. I hovered over her sweet little face and asked her to wake up. There wasn't a scratch on her, though she'd fallen right through the most horrible section of rocks. I kissed her on the cheek. *Marnie, Marnie, Marnie, it's Sam, what are you doing, let's get out of here.* Maybe she'd open her eyes and slap me or start laughing and cussing. I wanted to watch her face but she was vulnerable to the cold, so I covered her up as well as I could, stuck my gloves on her hands, and continued to wait and scream for help. Her loud snoring sounds were eerie, deep within her chest, but at least that was breathing, I told myself, so of course she'd be okay.

Out of nowhere a ranger in a black jacket appeared. He clicked out of his skis. "Hi, I'm . . . Tom?" he said, his voice rising, like he wasn't sure of his name. "What happened?"

"She crashed, she fell, she fell through all the rocks up there, she hit ice and trees, and she's unconscious."

"Are you serious? Really?" he said, looking confused, eyes wide with terror. He wanted to help but he didn't know how. He had no radio, and didn't know what to do at all, zero. We stood there like two helpless fools. I tried not to bark orders and insult him. He was frightened beyond belief, actually shaking; his pale, washed-out face nearly green. He took off his mittens and put on surgical gloves, took one step toward Marnie, and fell 10 feet down to the next tree.

"How could you not have a radio?"

"Rangers don't get issued walkie-talkies," he said, struggling to his feet, climbing back up. "The mountain can't afford it."

I uncovered Marnie's face so he could see her. What was the point?

After another round of screaming for help, Tom and I

stood in complete silence with our backs to each other, staring at the trees, the snow, Marnie's contorted figure splayed out in the snow. Time stretched out, felt like forever. Eventually ski patrol appeared. First one, then another. Bren and Bret. *How long has she been like this? Did you see her fall? How did it happen? Were you with her? Who are you? What's her name? Where are her skis?* A third patrolman with a sled crept down Satan's Maw from the top, trying not to crash himself, as runaway oxygen canisters jetted by us. His nametag said Brent.

I rejammed my skis into the snow to support the sled. They straightened out her body, and on the count of three slid her onto a flat plastic board and strapped her down. They lifted her onto the sled, covered her up with blankets, and said the gurgling sound might be a collapsed lung. They all skied down, slowly. One led, holding onto the handles of the sled, sliding ever so carefully, too steep to even snow-plow. Another guy held onto the rear with a rope, keeping everything steady. I was supposed to follow but I just stood there. I'd catch up in a second. I couldn't believe Marnie was inside that little cocoon. It should have been me; I was the reckless one, the crash-meister, the head-banger of trees. She was more cautious, showed better judgement. I skied down, repulsed by snow. When I got to the parking lot, she was already in the ambulance—ordinary life all around us. An angry father stormed ahead of his crying son and shouted that he'd *had it up to here.* With a stiff hand, the temperamental dad, who wore a green iridescent one-piece (picture a six-foot lizard in orange boots), indicated a line just above his nose.

A fire chief tapped me on the shoulder, told me to ride with him to the hospital. He ushered me into a red captain's truck. I'd never met a fire chief before. I felt honored, like I was in a sad American play about small towns. If only it was snowing again, then I could just stand behind the fire station and let three inches accumulate on my head—maybe the falling snow would forgive me or reverse what was happening. But there were no snowflakes falling anywhere. The fire chief seemed like the sweetest man in the universe, and why shouldn't he be, a man of approximately 60 who drank coffee all day long until bedtime. He looked like Captain Friendly, with a huge boozer nose and big sad eyes. How often had he been through this exact routine?

"I hope your friend's okay," he said. "What's her name?"

"Marnie." I got hopeful and increasingly ill. I stared out the windshield. I didn't know what to say. "How long have you worked for the fire department?" I asked.

"Forever," he said, "thirty-five years." He steered the truck. A tiny smile came and went. "I'm just helping out today. Shuttling folks. Today's busier than usual."

I could've told the fire chief that I'd always wanted to be a fireman myself. That I used to sleep in my clothes, and I made great lasagna. We said goodbye, shook hands. A few horrible steps across the icy hospital parking lot, and then the automatic doors swung open. I'd been to Mammoth Hospital as a teenager with a 12-inch hematoma on my thigh; a doctor slit me open and drained my blackened blood into a bucket like a mechanic changing oil.

A smiling receptionist held out a pen, asked me to sign in, which I did. Then I took a seat beside a gang of rat boys who were waiting for their bro Casey who was being treated for a broken wrist. One kid, whose face looked like it'd been bashed in more than once, his two front teeth missing, said, "The fool gets a foot off the ground and he thinks he's Shawn Palmer."

A minute later, a nurse called out my name, escorted me to a tiny room, asked me if Marnie was my wife or girlfriend, and could I contact her family. She said Marnie was in critical condition. I got her parents' phone number through Pittsburgh directory assistance. P-u-u-s-e-m-p, the only Puusemps in Pittsburgh. Marnie used to rave about the

Warhol Museum. I vacillated between full-throttle hysterics and an eerie composure. Both extremes disgusted me. When I wasn't weeping, I felt like a hollow creep, and when I sobbed out of control, I was nervous that a nurse would enter the room and see me quivering and ruined.

Before I had a chance to dial the phone number, there was a knock on the door. A female voice said the doctor would like to see me. I was up and out of the room in seconds. I felt a sickly pride that the lord of the hospital would ask or tell me anything, and that I was the diplomat of Marnie's country. The doctor was a compact, little man with big reassuring eyes. He introduced himself as John Smith. We shook hands. He said he had to drill two holes into Marnie's head to relieve brain pressure, that the swelling was so severe she would've died within minutes. A spinning laughter whirled inside my stomach. Holes? Drilled? I couldn't help thinking, What is this, woodshop? That's a little too primitive for my friend. I stared at the doctor. Maybe I said thank you. A nurse moved me back into the room with the phone. Two minutes later, I was telling Mrs. Puusemp that Marnie was involved in a ski accident, that she was unconscious from a head injury, that a surgeon just drilled holes into her head, that they were flying her to Reno, that her head trauma was too severe for this little mountain hospital. Mrs. Puusemp was remarkably calm. She took down my phone number, hung up, phoned her husband, and called me back with him on the other line, asking questions. He wanted to know if her brains had spilled out. I said they had not, that everything was intact except for the two holes.

The helicopter pilot was right there in the hallway eating a McDonald's hamburger. He took a huge bite, held up a finger, chewed twice, swallowed, and said there was no way I could hitch a ride to Reno, too much weight. My appetite returned in a flash when I smelled his French fries.

A kid named Shane Miller who worked at the hospital as

a nutritionist heard all this from down the hall and asked if I needed a ride home. He looked familiar. I recognized him from the cover of *Powder* magazine. We walked to his truck.

"Nasty shit, man. That girl Marnie's your girlfriend or something?" He had big dark eyes, huge eyelashes, and thick lips.

"No, she's a friend, like a close pal, but not my girlfriend."

"Damn." Shane looked like a tall Sophia Loren without boobs. "Where to?"

"Motel 6."

"Ah, the 6, I've partied there. They have a sweet Ja-coose. 109 degrees if no one fucks with the temp." Each time Shane shifted into another gear, the trucked lurched and blurted a loud clacking sound, throwing both of us into the dash-board. "I've seen your friend ski. She rips."

"Yeah, I know. I just got off the phone with her mother."

"Harsh, bro." He turned a corner. "You want a bong hit?"

"I'm good." I noticed a headless Barbie doll on the seat between us, 666 written in black marker across her stomach.

Shane's truck skidded into the motel lot. I ran to my room, changed clothes, dove onto the incredibly squeaky motel bed, and assembled two peanut butter, salami, and pickle sandwiches on rye. I threw all of Marnie's belongings into her duffel bag, and all of my crap into my bag, checked out of the motel, and drove two dismal hours north. David Bowie on the radio sounded like the prophet of hope. I drove through a quiet town called Lee Vining. No stop signs, everything closed. One gas station, a café called *Hi, Let's Eat*. And 50 miles later, Bridgeport, where I once visited my Mammoth friend Zach who spent a month in the town's modest jail for stealing a car, driving drunk, and whatever other outstanding warrants were in the police computer. Zach wrote the word *incarcerate* on his skis. He said the jail-ers made good pizza.

The Intensive Care Unit in Reno was filled with fucked-up

white people who'd shot each other. Hardcore skinheads with swastikas on their jackets and various other earthlings drifted in to pay one another a visit. And cops. A TV was on with the sound off. After a while, Marnie's parents walked in. I'd met them once before at school. Mrs. Puusemp looked a lot like Marnie, only shorter, the same freckly cheeks and blue-gray eyes, the same middle-western, nasal voice. The father looked like Ernest Hemingway, a big burly dude with a wide face and a white beard. They were smiling. We embraced. In a flash, the three of us were sobbing. Mr. Puusemp told me not to blame myself and to promise never to ski without a helmet. He and his wife walked over to a wall phone and identified themselves as Marnie's parents to an unseen security guard who eventually buzzed them both in. I waited in the lobby.

That night I stayed in my own hotel room adjacent to the hospital. Marnie's parents insisted I be their guest. They bought me breakfast, lunch, and dinner, and when other friends showed up the following day, they received equal generosity. Marnie was in a coma, but her brain swelling was relatively stable. She responded to questions with blinks. She knew she was 29, not 30. She cried a lot. She was in a lot of pain. A tiny physical therapist came on the scene and put her through a daily routine of arm and leg exercises, and she instructed us on how to do the same when we were alone with Marnie so her muscles wouldn't atrophy. I massaged her feet and told her about the neo-Nazis in the lobby. I kissed her on the nose and was certain her eyes would open. At one point she yawned. She looked like a spiritual leader with her shaved head. We all took turns reading her the huge pile of faxed letters that poured in from every aunt, uncle, neighbor, old schoolmate, and teacher. We played her favorite girl groups on a CD player—Elastica, Veruca Salt, and the Go-Gos. Her father slipped me a point n' shoot camera and insisted I take pictures of Marnie and all her surroundings, which I did constantly, even if it felt intrusive and morbid. The patient next to her was a man who shot himself in the head after killing his wife. His head swelled to the size of a pumpkin. When Marnie's cubicle got crowded, I'd wander over to his partitioned area. On one occasion his arm mysteriously rose like he was saluting Hitler.

Every night Marnie's father sequestered himself in a room and delivered a meticulous progress report into an outgoing voice mail so people could call in and find out her daily status. He took copious notes on exactly what the doctors said regarding infectious diseases, inner-cranial pressure, and brain stem functions, and relayed that into the tape recorder. At the end of each day, Mom and Dad and whoever else was visiting piled into a tiny room equipped with a desk, a speaker phone, and one chair, and listened to hours of phone messages left by people who wished them well. I sat on the floor and stared at my feet and listened as each call generated strong reactions around the room. Mr. Puusemp, one of the tougher 50-year-old men I'd ever met, someone who could easily tear the arms off most guys half his age, was by far the most emotional. When he wasn't weeping profusely, struggling to catch his breath, he'd tell stories or ask me what I thought of his spur of the moment ski helmet design he drew on a cocktail napkin. He was a super successful entrepreneur obsessed with solving problems. He'd sit me down in the hospital cafeteria and ask me how I could come up with the perfect artwork that would enchant the world and make me rich. You have to start with what people need most right now, he'd say, and I'd stumble through the conversation saying incoherent things about organic process and intuition. I told him about my paintings of male robots, how they looked like the Michelin Man with lengthy word balloons about needing a blowjob, while my female robots, with their pink backgrounds and streamline Metropolis-like curves, only thought about science. I was kind of in awe of Mr. Puusemp. His interest in who I was, how I was making a living (construction, pounding nails), made me nervous. It was like talking to a senator. He really did seem lit up from the inside. More than once he pulled a little rubber mouse out of his pocket and playfully terrorized an unsuspecting nurse. If she didn't respond favorably to the mouse gag, he didn't want her handling his daughter. His sense of humor was relentless, the only thing that kept us from sinking. I accidentally slammed a car door on his thumb. Without a shriek, he calmly asked me to open the car door.

At the end of one long day and night, all Marnie's pals from L.A. crowded into the hospital hotel room like at a slumber party and smoked pot and drank Jack Daniel's. The hotel didn't even allow cigarettes. At some point the phone rang and it was Mr. Puusemp in his room on another floor. He'd gotten word of our misbehavior and asked us to stop. He used the expression *tout de suite.*

I returned home and started keeping a journal for Marnie. I yacked on endlessly about what went on every day she was out. I made whoever I was with throw in a few words of their own, even if they'd never met her. I got it in my head that I should do everything that Marnie thought was cool, so I dyed my hair blue, bought trail running shoes, ran in Elysian Park, pumped iron, did zillions of sit-ups and push-ups, played tennis, swam laps at the Y, ate Indian food, and pizza, went to more parties than I could stomach, drank champagne, read *Infinite Jest* by David Foster Wallace, tried to remember jokes I'd heard and retell them with some conviction like her dad (her idol), took lots of photographs, made piles of drawings, and fucked every cute girl willing to take her clothes off. I even golfed. I hate golf. I taped a tiny snapshot of Marnie to the tip of my skis, bought a helmet, glopped a ton of white paint on it and then a sloppy black snowflake, skied three or four days a week, and nearly got caught in an avalanche. After seven hours of skiing on St. Patrick's Day, I got a call from Mr. Puusemp. I was staying at a friend's cabin in Mammoth. We were in constant phone contact. He told me that Marnie had died the previous night. I was standing in the hallway, staring at a ceramic Santa Claus. I was wearing these clownish snowboard pants Marnie had bought me for my birthday. She'd been in a coma for 10 weeks. Her doctors weren't sure what kind of shape she'd be in, if she'd ever be able to think or walk or talk if she did come out of the coma. On her most productive day of physical therapy, Mr. Puusemp said, she willed herself away. He said that it was just like her to do that, to take control of the situation—if she couldn't be physically active, she didn't want to live.

A week later, my blue-haired brain delivered a eulogy in the largest church in Pennsylvania to a zillion people who adored Marnie as much as I did. I told a story about the time she took me on my first backpacking trip through the Sierras. I was a complete novice and didn't know squat. I'd never slept outside before. After a 10-mile hike through a high alpine canyon we stopped at a lake. She wanted to swim naked. She asked me if I'd mind, her swimming naked. I said no, that it would be all right. I'd guard the lake, make sure no one saw. She stripped. I could feel her naked over my shoulder, giggling. Out of stupidity or some psycho brotherly respect, I didn't turn my head. I closed my eyes and pictured my sexy naked friend standing on a flat rock. Then I heard a big splash.

TIPS
FROM
THE
SENSUAL MAN

TIPS FROM THE SENSUAL MAN

Do not lay on top of your mate like a dead stone. To avoid squashing, distribute bulk onto your elbows. This allows both parties ample pelvic movement. Caress entire body. Start at the toes and work your way up to the head area. Lick between each individual toe. Partners like that. Lick your way up the thigh but don't leave a snail trail. Break up journey with dry terse kisses. Approach the anus with caution. Kiss and grip the butt cheeks but do not under any circumstances pull the cheeks apart and root. At the right moment it can be highly erotic for your partner to be on their stomach, legs spread, and have their anus lightly licked. You will see that the anus is shut tight and doesn't appear to want company. Not so. With your tongue you can say, "Hey, you shy eye socket, no one's going to hurt you," and soon enough it will relax, and the rusty door will creak open. Do not poke. During intercourse, be creative and peruse outside the anus with a lone finger and tenderly insert it into the hole itself. The sensual man does not put it in deeper than an inch. Don't twist, wiggle, or rotate. The point of having a finger inside the anus is to massage the anal wall. Think of an underwater bass player. Handling a woman's breasts is very tricky. Do not squeeze. Lick them with the tip of your tongue, but do not make a mess. A bosom is not food. Do not slobber. Don't spend too much time on one breast. Alternate, left to right. Under no circumstances should you chew, gnaw, or suckle. Remember, you are not nursing. Next is breathing, kissing, and licking ears. Be aware of your saliva. Breathe through your nose even when your mouth is open. You don't want to huff out a blast of sour exhaust. Kissing. Do not flop your fat wet cow tongue into partner's mouth. Form tongue into a point and probe with subtle curiosity, similar to how an insect would investigate with its feelers. Do not swab the teeth, gums, or throat. Apply the pointed tongue principle to the ears. The ear is sensitive. A whispered word or slurp can sound like a satanic explosion. Licking the nostril induces a repulsive aquatic sensation. If you feel you are reaching orgasm too soon, take a deep breath and think about the horrors of the world: slaughter, train derailments, worms eating out donkey's eyes, or mundane things like gas and electric bills, laundry, bank, phone Mom, or think of something neutral like solar energy. You must breathe or you will die. After ejaculation, do not immediately dismount. Remain in position for 60 seconds. Allow the pot roast time to cool. Remain silent. Do not say wow, thank you, or I'm sorry. Not even I love you, which can have a disastrous effect. Allow the miracle of time to work its magic. No television. No bathroom, even if you have to (easily taken as a hostile gesture). Lie there like you are in a trance. Sighing is good. Caress partner's belly. Kiss belly. Kiss face area. Follow these tried and true methods and you'll be a superlative and sought after lover.

PINK SLIP OF WOOD

As you know, you're a well-respected man in the department, but you've got this circus-style organ between your legs and I just think you should be aware of the fact that your colleagues envy the Helen of Troy out of you, and by that I mean that you've reduced all the men on the 32nd floor into high-pitched dolls, as if we've all had sex changes, or like we've been psychologically neutered; once upon a time we were big growling lions grazing the lush landscape, but now, as the daily mythology builds around you, we find ourselves not man enough to lick the adhesive side of envelopes. We are not quite sure what the longterm effects are, how the presence and knowledge of you will affect us in five, fifteen years down the line, but what we do know is that there are intimidation factors that need to be addressed immediately, issues of morale and self-confidence; there's genuine fear in the faces of formerly ferocious individuals. The idea of *being a man*, and the inverse, the whole complex notion of *not being man enough*—it's an abstract concept, to be sure, as much as you can be sure of something you're unable to lock down and understand—but we're going to have to let you go. W-w-with deep regret, we're going to have to say bon voyage, w-w-which is unfortunate (I have trouble with my W's—I used to stutter when I was a kid, now it's back) because you're a fine employee, a team player, as they say. You see, the whole giant organ thing is negatively affecting the workplace environment. There was a time when the guys looked up to me as the largest thing since the Louisville Slugger. I once inspired awe and fantasy. It was not uncommon for the guys to mill around the water cooler on Monday morning and discuss their sexual success stories and say they were thinking of me—similar to how football players conjure up Knut Rockney to inspire them to greater levels of performance—that images of Kafka (that's my member's name) drifted into their thoughts during intercourse; Kafka thought he was a large beetle that couldn't quite reach the doorknob of his bedroom and walk or crawl out. Now, I did some research on the beetle and discovered that the beetle in *The Metamorphosis* is a species that has wings. What I'm trying to say is that the penis could've flown right out the window and gone to work or school or wherever the hell that unhappy Jewish guy didn't want to go. All guys name their genitals. First my mother was calling my thing Ding Dang Do. A bad name regardless of its musical appeal. My father called it Samson. He called his own penis The Lizard, and whenever he had to take a leak he'd say, time to walk The Lizard. Creepy, but now that he's passed on any sight of a reptile sends me into an emotional desert. Since I'm a bookish type and my favorite writer is Kafka, I thought Kafka would be best for me since most sexual encounters are filled with doubt, confusion, and an infinity of paralyzing dread. For a while I considered calling him Gregor but that sounded a little too granular. Last I heard you were calling your member Area 54. I love the concept, but that's just my point—straining to be one of the guys. Coming up with the perfect nickname. I'm man enough to concede when a bigger tool shows up that can do the job better, but the problem is that your crank is giving everyone nightmares. The guys are waking up screaming in the middle of the night. No one is sleeping. Everyone's drinking buckets of coffee and then falling asleep in front of their computer and a little later barking their way out of daymares. We spoke to a horse doctor and he said that we need to get rid of *the demon-stud.* Productivity is way down and this is all during the Viagra era so we're all hard but not really up for the challenge. Envy is dangerous, it chokes the victim. There's actually less oxygen to breathe, we're gasping—and it logically follows that we'd blame the thing we worship, you, our genital deity, after blaming ourselves, our respective gene pools, and God himself, of course, always an easy target, but in the end there's no one to blame but you, O Cocklord. We were fine before you stepped in and dwarfed our gentle giants. A businessman must never drool. Robert, Bobby, John, and the other Bob are cramming cotton puffs in between their gums and lips to keep the saliva where it belongs, not pooling around our tasseled loafers. You have little eyes, the skull of a T-Rex, and this turbo sperm log which has frankly made us all a bit suicidal. You know how a big cock enters the brain—no, you probably don't know this, and can't comprehend a word I'm saying—a bigass dong barrels in the side door of the normal male brain and camps out like a belligerent elephant, refusing to budge. In another life I hope to be a zookeeper for your cage and mop up all the dick sauce your lower half discharges. Most of us work 18 hours a day and box the clown to slo-mo close-ups of one fleshhead sucking on another. But in this current life, this tedious humiliating strip of tightly wound cable, we can't even accomplish that. Now, the simple relaxing j.o. session has been stolen from our lives, which is another way of saying, mental grand larceny. Granted, we're surging in the dollars dept., we all own mucho real estate, but no plot of land can match up to the 20-plus inches of erectile furor you're packing. Look at you. You're shy, humble, polite—you flop your meat down right between your toes as natural as pie. We don't want love. What we want is a bigger, more substantial chunk to suds up in the shower and adjust during tiresome luncheons. And, if at a party, having had a bit too much to drink, we find ourselves in a closet with a coworker, we unleash the Salisbury battering ram, an instant standing ovation, which in turn leads to awe, respect, overall happiness, salvation, and peace for all.

As you must know, or maybe you don't, the last thing on the mind of a fellow with a big thing are the little people— you can't hide a joystick. They broadcast their own diminution. Don't nod your head. Now is not a good time to agree with me. Of course one can hide it. They go into hiding on their own. They know things. They're ducking for cover, committing the lower halves of our bodies to a life of chaff by squirming into the flesh bunker. To seek shelter only screams of fear, and most walking, talking, breathing human beings, like other predators, can smell that sour panic like hot sloppy lunch, and find the cowering soldier in seconds, sandwiched between thighs. What all of your colleagues are now forced to do is march straight into the boardroom, strip, jump face-first on the table, flip over, go spread-eagle, and say here's what I am, a minute steak, a tough little fillet that means business. Act proud, know your limitations, remember names. The phrase I *won't take no for an answer* only works if you mean it, if you're willing to cut your own balls off. I tell my fellow genital mates, leave your balls on. Live your life. But I stray from the singular purpose of these thoughts: You and your thick pylon have thrown the company into chaos. The planet earth, the ground we're accustomed to treading on, is no longer there. Instability reigns, and you know what that means. We'll have to say goodbye to you. You're overqualified. I know this is sudden and not an easy thing to accept; it's hard on all of us, but let me tell you plain and simple, it's been a lot harder on me than it has on you. And please don't take yourself to a surgeon and get a shaft reduction. All that will do is make us look at you in disbelief. What was once a man with Guinness Book–type numbers is now half a man, a fool, someone who'll diminish his Johnson in order to get his cool corporate job back. That won't solve the problem. Take your personal monument that I assume never gets completely hard, that droops and flops like a groggy amphibian—I'm sorry, that was uncalled for— and go. Some of us are running out of gas on the interstate, afraid to visit a service station to refuel, because the 10-foot hoses wrapped around the pumps remind us of you. It's costing us time and money. We're pulling up to the full ser- vice bay, rolling down the window with our eyes closed, and shouting, *fill it*, to the attendant. No more 10-foot hoses. This is madness. Leave our building and never return. Your cock is not like a baby's arm or a third leg; it's like some other type of entity or peninsula, and we just can't have that here. I'm terribly sorry. Don't even think of shaking my hand, just go, and please, stop crying.

TWINS

People, not just guys, have sex fantasies about my sister and I because we're twins and we model lingerie. That would make a certain amount of sense. Since we were created in the same package and we're always photographed together, guys believe they're entitled to the double set. They start out with one, and then they beg for two. We say, Uh uh, sorry, no good, not moral, bad, because we believe in *you know who* above our apartment, clouds, planet, and, we think, the entire solar system basically; and somewhere in the Bible, we're not really sure what page, it says two girls, especially two sexually active twin sisters, should never lay down with the same guy no matter how much we love each other and no matter how many treats the guy promises us and that includes trips to Bali. We never use God's name in vain, and we're not going to do it now. It can get pretty confusing. We sometimes call him HIM—the inspiration for everything that's ever been done, from the reading of a hymnal on Sunday morning to a climb on the Himalayas.

Guy-swaggering is a cover-up for the yawning need for

giant spoonfuls of reassurance, Mommy stuff, and little rubby-rubs on the head. We strip and the boy-bull stops scraping the ground with his hooves, he stops breathing. They get all intimidated because we're professionals, we do special things with our eyes, and sometimes we don't smile because that's sexier, but it's also scary. For sure it's complicated, like science. What is inside us exactly beside cells, organs, and gunk? Since we were born with perfect exteriors and we're professional models, guys want to get inside us and rummage around, explore our little caves (mouth, vagina, and anus, *ouch*), not very echoey. Our Jeeps each have a bumper sticker that says, I *(heart)* MY VAGINA, because it's true, we do love them. We shave them into the most petite little stingers so our laby lips are bare like a newborn's cherina (that's one of our nicknames for it).

Just because we model bustiers and teddies, everyone thinks we are sex experts, like porn stars. Shatter that myth. We're sexual fumblers. A guy will say harder or faster and we do it too hard or too fast or not hard or fast enough, and when he says suck or jerk we always lick too softly or hold it wrong or stab the urethra with our nails. When referring to more than one urethra you say ure*thrae*. When guys say, Flip over girls (okay, so we do fuck the same guys, oh shit, we're going to hell), we usually kick them in the head with our high heels because they always insist that we keep our shoes on so that we look exactly like our pictures. So the guy is holding his face and moaning *ouwee* and we're apologizing, saying sorry sorry how embarrassing, but there's no recovery. It's like, who brought in the bad comedians? Their head hurts, they want to go home.

Our favorite movie is *Shoah*. A gentleman of the Jewish persuasion took us to it. Eight hours long, one movie, the tickets were $20 each, took us two days to watch. We got a terrible feeling looking at the popcorn machine—very morbid—cooking, confinement, bursting kernels. We bought a large, but out of respect for the dead and our date, whose name will remain a secret, we didn't eat a single morsel. Maybe we had a few bites in the lobby, but five minutes into the movie our date wouldn't stop crying. Popcorn used to be our favorite food. Now we throw up when we see a forested landscape. When we see beauty we want to know what's hidden. When the war ended the clergy removed portraits of Hitler and put up the almighty HIM, but the walls had discolored, the frames were smaller, and no one could forget the previous face. Women can be Nazis too, but it's men who cut off heads, gloat, and experiment on flesh. A woman's offensive is economic, nonviolent. We isolate the enemy, boycott businesses, and distribute literature. We fight with our minds. It's strange what you have to do to a penis, the same thing all the time. Suck and jerk. We want something less abrupt, less pistonlike. Something seamless and unbroken. Maybe we're lesbians. Maybe we're not. Our favorite sexual position is 69ing each other while the guy is loving us doggie; that way we can see the guy's balls going clang-clang like hairy tea bags. And if his iguana comes out we can kiss it before escorting it back in.

ENCHANTED FOREST

The lumberjack with the leaf-green eyes, cherry-red lips, heavy-duty Master padlock earrings, and two-day stubble bristling on his rosy cheeks like a blooming cactus, strode up to the counter bowlegged, unstrapped his huge, ultra-sharp axe, gently slammed it to the floor, and said, "I'll have the usual," in a voice softer than feathers.

The expression on my face worried me: eyes several inches bugged out of their sockets, ears burning well over a hundred degrees Fahrenheit, stomach knotting, drool pooling. I looked down and drew a little question mark on the order pad, and then a whole row of them. Everything in me was stirring. If he saw my pencil moving maybe he'd think I was writing down a specific meal.

"My apologies for ordering the *usual*. I'll spell out my *usual* so there's no confusion," he said. "Steak and eggs, steak well, eggs over hard, six of them, please, with the yokes a tad runny if possible, which I understand might be medium, but medium often translates into a generally softer type of *easy* egg which I don't want any part of." His hair was black, eyes electric, follow-me-to-the-promised-land blue. "Sorry to be so fussy, a small stack of buttermilk pancakes, home fries, also grilled well, tomatoes, bacon, sausage, apple sauce, four slices of sourdough toast, nearly burnt, buttered like a dairy truck crashed into them, if you know what I mean."

I did know. At that moment I pictured a Carnation step van on Curly Ridge, careening out of control, up and over the guardrails, plunging down into the gorge 1000 feet below, slamming through the roof of Genoa Bakery. "Buttered beyond reason," I said. I wanted him to like me.

He nodded and his padlock earrings jiggled in unison. "I actually like it drippy," he said. "I need to bulk up. I'm losing weight from all the tree chopping." He poked at his ribs.

We shook hands and I instantly felt like a toddler. Big Poppa, take me home.

"My name's Zeus Lily. What's yours?"

I pointed to the name tag on my shirt, not quite ready to talk.

His eyes did a double take. "Well, you're my first Skeeter."

I walked back into the kitchen and stared at the ticket. First I wrote *well*, then I wrote *drippy*, then I drew a caricature of Zeus tickling a bunny rabbit, and then I threw a 32 oz. porterhouse on the grill, cracked six eggs two by two, and stared at the potatoes, bacon, and sausage, which were already made, and thought about giant crackling redwoods thumping to the ground and Mr. Lily's order and what it meant to me.

"That's a mile of man," I said. I was talking to myself. It couldn't be helped. "Do I drop to my knees and pray? What's the procedure for encountering wonders of the world?"

I ladled out pancake batter, put four pieces of sourdough in the toaster, grabbed a knife, and said, "Calm down, no more talking."

What if he finds out I'm not really Skeeter? I thought fretfully, no longer talking to myself.

"Just cook a perfect meal," I said loudly, unable to keep my trap shut for more than three seconds.

Shut up, I thought, you keep this bottom talk to yourself. Press your lips together now, pleasure the ultimate slab of man meat, nothing more. He will cut, gnash, tear, and swallow, then rise off his stool, tummy full, and digest in the forest like a sleepy bear. If I can only parlay this Epicurean highlight into a real-life dark-forest tryst starring me as pulverized entity in mattress of mud and thistle, and he the love gargantuan with anvil earrings, life would exceed previous expectations.

And then I wondered about our mutual loneliness. Maybe the lumberjack wants company. Zeus Lily has his trees and the forest and all the chipmunks and bullfrogs and eagles that trust him like a brother, father, super uncle, best friend. Maybe I'm loved, too, though I don't know by whom, and I just need a little convincing, someone to compile a list of wonderful things and show it to me every time they add five more cheerful items to prove how special my life has become. Observe the fry cook in the midst of a carnal seizure. I see myself underneath a mile of Zeus Lily foreskin, shaded from the bright, early-morning sun. Where am I? It is so dark at dawn. As soon as I began to peel back his heavy velvet curtain in my inter-cranial porno, the toaster dinged and sent me off the ground in surprise.

I buttered the lumberjack's bread, it's me who does it now, I thought, butters him up, slathers, greases, lubes. Never in my wildest dreams did I expect to make breakfast for a thing that was actually two large men poured into one monolith. I caught a peek of him through the serving window. All politeness and manners: straight military posture, napkin tucked into the neck of his Carhartt jacket, hands in lap, eyes closed, lashes fluttering as if deep in meditation. What finishing school did he attend? Delicate Ox Academy? His hands were triple the size of mine and his shoes seemed to be imported from the island of Tonga. "Penis," I said out loud, like someone injected with truth serum, and then caught myself and moved back into safe silent thinking, *penis, penis, penis.* My brain was flashing a love monster so big I nearly choked on my own thought.

I flipped the porterhouse, the eggs, and hotcakes.

O, how I live to butter his ass, his thick loggy legs, and giant veiny feet; and with utensils known as tongue, toes, and tip of nose, I sang silently to myself, *la la la, I shall butter his balls,* which I picture crushing my eyelids like two full-to-capacity duffel bags.

If I bark or yelp when hit by a typhoon of semen I hope he doesn't mind, I thought, as I raised the spatula to eye level and stared at a tear drop of grease. I do my best to purr. I am damp, perspiring, in the grip of slaughterhouse giddiness. Lily's thumbs appear swollen, gorilla-like. I could be happy just sucking on one of those, I thought, my brain swelling to capacity. That would be fine for a first date. He was scarred up in the temples and neck like worn rodeo leather, and squeaked ever so slightly as if a tiny hinge inside him needed oiling. I flopped the steak onto a three-foot serving tray, the eggs, cakes, spuds, tomatoes, toast, condiments, parsley, orange slices, and everything else, and brought it over to him on the far stool away from the cash register. Just as he nodded thanks, one of his earrings hit the sugar dispenser and shattered a zillion pieces everywhere. We looked at each other, both of us startled. Zeus Lily opened his mouth to a perfect O shape.

"I'm terribly sorry," he said. "I'm like an oil barge slamming into a butterfly house."

"No you're not. I mean, yes you are. I mean, let me fetch a broom." I ran for one in the corner and started sweeping. Sugar looks pretty interesting on the floor, especially mixed in with broken glass that kind of resembles diamonds if you want it to. Zeus Lily slid his breakfast to the right and moved one stool over. He watched me sweep.

"Skeeter, how much do you weigh?"

"140, maybe."

"Would that be soaking wet?"

"What?"

"Never mind." He put a huge square of steak in his mouth and started to chew, the fork in his hand looked like a Barbie utensil from her miniature tea party set. "You know, Skeeter, most of the lumberjacks I chop trees with are homosexuals, myself included."

I dropped the broom.

"That's the spirit. Now why don't you throw down that apron and join us? We sleep in the forest together. We're happy."

"What do you mean, happy?"

"I mean, we're not depressed." He took a bite of egg and potato. "We're big men. We're doing work we love. We're out in nature. And we have sex with each other most nights and no one gets overly jealous."

"That sounds like a pretty good situation," I said, sweeping the last bits into a dustpan.

"What do you think, Skeeter, care to walk out of here arm in arm and become one of the lumberjacks?"

"I do."

"We're not getting married, you know, we're just going to chop trees and live as one."

"I understand," I said, and untied my apron and looped it over a hook on the wall. "Do I have to wear a plaid shirt?"

"Yes," he said. "First we'll go shopping, then we'll go into the forest." He stood up and reached for my hand. "That was a lovely meal you made me, little buddy. Thank you."

"You're very welcome."

DEAR APRÈS-SKI FORUM

1.

Ja, hello, good American. My English is better when I speak. Writing is hard, so bear with me (do not hesitate to hand me the Blue Ribbon when my skillful pun steals the show). Ha ha, anyway, I am the big blond German guy. That's what I emanate as a presence to people when they inquire as to what they are to look for when they go hunting for my countenance when I have a date blind or something and anyhow this is very new for me, to scribble down what I have done as a sexual person, but I will do my best, because as Freud would say, Cock spiel das gut for die Herz und Gemut, or at least as a story at the table of tomorrow which belongs to your Schneeflocke kultur. I paraphrase the good Doktor because he liked sex and was the first to make talking dirty a science. Contrary to popular belief some Germans are shy and I am one of those type of fellows. One thing that makes me withdraw slightly is my size. I am two meters tall. I can barely fit through a doorway because my shoulders are quite wide. Apparently the ladies like that. They also like strong young arm I have between mein tree-truck legs. Und so, one afternoon I was riding up the Gondola and at the midway station three American Fraus with blond hair stormed into my tight little quarters. They are wearing lots of makeup, you see. Suddenly we were 100 meters off the ground, and the Gondola stopped. I joked, I have one final request und that is to . . . and oh boy, they were naked quickly and not a moment went by when there was not a shaved pussy, a round milk maid boobie, or belly ring in my face, or a wiggling tongue in my mouth, on my cock, or in my rectum and Stromschnelle, to be precise—and as my favorite American band Pavement would sing, "Hi-ho sil-ver ride." What I did with my Deutchcock was routine; I was only following orders memorized from Grandpa Heiner's porno-cinemas I watched as a frolicking youth-boy. In und out like madness, destroying city after city, screams and shouts, bombs und fire. Schnell, I commanded, as explosions and girls cried and sang and they laugh wicked like private parade with giant artificial keys presented by the mayor which was me and then the girls acting out the communist revolution in reverse with their tight behinds which I swallowed and squashed like a pirate—oh man, sometimes I feel like a dragon, especially after they gulped what seemed like six pints of my man sea und hairy kelp and wanting more, groaning yes, yes. I whispered, lick my goddamn balls, as the courteous uniformed employee handed over the skis to the female guests who were suddenly back to normal (Gondola repaired)—mein snowboard is unstrapped from the rack which in the summertime holds the mountain bicycles. I am a board-head (that is slang for snowboarder), I am postmodern guy. Snowboard is today and now and I don't believe in my grandparent's past. Okay? I say, So long girls. I wave goodbye.

2.

I'm a wilderness girl meaning I like to drop trou in the trees
rather than walk into the lodge to remove my gear. I am also
a highly sexual person. I tire my boyfriend out. Me, several
times a day. He, once or twice. I was on the USC Race Team
in college. We were terrible but we loved partying in the
mountains. God, I love my computer. I just wanted to say
that. It's so cute, more obedient than any puppy dog. I take
it to bed with me; it blinks when it's sleeping, and says,
Goodnight, Pumpkin. So anyway, here's what happened to me
and it's 100 percent true so prepare yourself for something a
little sexy. I'm skiing, okay, and I had to pee real bad. So I
cruised over to Fresno Bowl, a place where I've done
Number Ones before without any interruption. So there I
am, my purple pants down at my ankles, squatting and peeing, picturing a deep yellow hole in the snow, admiring a
trio of lady bugs, when suddenly, surprise! this hunky stud
boy appeared in a red jacket with a white cross. O fuck, ski
patrol. Bust-ed. I'm not known for being a fan of young
meat; I'm not a cradle robber, but there he was, a clean
shaven, creamy dreamy blue-eyed delight. I said, Hi. And he
said, You're peeing. I said, Excuse me? I always do that even
though I knew what he said. It's a bad habit that drives my
sisters crazy, but I can't help it anyway. So he says again,
You're peeing, and then he says, Your ass sure looks sweet.
And I said, You want some? And he says, Fuck yeah. So I
stand up and stop peeing, and he screams, No, I mean, I
want some of your water, why don't you piss on me? So I'm
like, whoa, can't believe my ears; I always wanted to piss on
my boyfriend and have him drench me in a golden shower
but of course he's not into water sports because he's such a
conservative loser. I've got to break up with him before
2005. All right, come over here, I tell him, what's your name?
He side-steps over, clicks out of his skis, and says, John, but

my friends call me Bumpy. I say, Wow, what a cool name. He goes, Yeah. Then he pulls down his pants. Wicked-looking cock you got there, I tell him, mind if I munch? Hell, I don't mind, he says, as long as you piss on me at some point, or else I'll clip your pass . . . just kidding. I lift up his cock and there are the droopiest testicles I've ever seen in my life. Like halfway to his knees. Balls like I've never seen. Are you part octopus? I asked, as I began licking the search-and-rescue expert. No, I'm Irish, he said; and then he said, Squeeze the fucker, just grip the freak with all your might and then bite it. So I did that for a while, and then he screams, Oh, mother of God, and blasts the works down my throat . . . whatever, fucking on the snow would've been tricky. He tasted like a broccoli. Kind of like oceanic wheat grass. Then he lies down and says, Spray me, baby. So I redrop trou and tinkle out what remains in my bladder, right in his mouth. Oh yeah, he says, World Cup tequila, give me more. I grab his ears and grind my pelvis into his mouth. Then I start riding his nose, first slowly to make sure he's into it, and when I hear him groan in a positive manner and mumble something, I crank the volume full blast and totally go off on his face and clitpound the poor boy. He hangs with me to the bitter end. I'm not fast. A cloud descends on us and it begins to snow. I get off his face and huge snowflakes float from the sky and land on his wet face. You look like a glazed donut, I say. Dusted with sugar, he says. Then I lie on my back and watch the big flakes fall slo-mo, very psychedelic. He stands over me and goes for it right in my face, a torrent of hot yellow, 98.6 degrees, at least 30 seconds worth. I close my eyes, the spray is insane. When he's done he offers me a handkerchief. How sweet. I decline, lick my lips, unzip my chest pocket, pull out a doob, and fire it up. One puff by Bumpy bleeds it down to a roach. Our minds are baked, our hearts . . . hmm. I stood up, lightheaded. Time to make some turns. We got back on our skis. All right, X-Screams, he said, how do you like them? They're killer, I say, how do you like your Bandits? Sweet, he said, lifting up the tail of his right ski. Cool, we kind of said together, like we were totally in sync, me, blushing like a freak. I take off. Snow so fine. He follows. Tear it up, Little Ripper, he yells. No one's ever called me that.

3.

When my sorority planned a ski trip I had no idea I was in for such a rowdy carnal encounter. I told my girlfriends, I don't swallow sperm. They looked at me like I was insane. There's pressure from every side. The world insists that I rejoice in it, that I swallow the gross glop, smack my lips, and ask for another helping. But anyway, what's a Gondola? The Puffs, that's the name of our group, they said. You're lucky we're letting you come along, stupid prude. I swear . . . I like guys, I just don't think it's cool if they cum in your mouth. Why should I have to swallow something that isn't really nutritious? My objection is I don't like squishy foods, old bananas, custards, or any type of thick, room temp beverages. But I hear sperm is good for your complexion, so that's what I'll do. I'll massage it into my skin if I have to. I hate this entire flow of words but I might as well continue. What happened to me is . . . I was riding up the Gondola (is that Italian for something?) with five big men. Out of the blue, no provocation from me, they all pull their cocks out and start masturbating. I was just looking out the window, minding my own business, but then I got this sudden curiosity, maybe I won't hate it. Maybe spode tastes good. I eat a lot of fast foods. I like lots of salt on my popcorn, maybe boy jizz is really salty like that, and since five guys are masturbating in this Gondola contraption, I might as well have a European adventure at this Mammoth Resort, and sample; plus I'm on vacation and a wild experience is something I promised myself this weekend. I just kind of kneeled in the center and let it all happen. One guy named Bob said he was ready to *shoot*. I said, Don't use that terminology, please, violent guys are a turnoff. He apologized and said, Quick cash. That's better, I said. Then another guy who introduced himself as Robert stood up and said, Fry that thing. Bob came on my shoulder and Robert in my hair. Fabulous. Then the other Bob, who had the queerest method of doing himself, like he was trying to jimmy open a broken door, dripped out a morsel and said, Crawl home. I just looked at him like, What is your problem? Two more remained. Rick screamed, Oh my shit hell, and came on one of the Bobs who started unpleasantly cussing, and someone named Bill tapped his massive tool on my brow. He had a twisty vein that looked like an access road on a wrinkled map—I jerked him out the window. He shouted, Nobody knows me. Translucent sperm-ropes swirled down to earth. Boy, did he seem sad. Our ride was over; the lovely sky boat docked at the top of the mountain. All that sperm and not one droplet crossed my lips. We got out of the Gondola a little dazed, but psyched and ready to rock, or at least they were. I was frightened. The young Gondolier handed me my skis with the little roosters on the tips. What do I do now? Everything appeared so treacherous. How am I going to get down the mountain? Where are my girlfriends? Maybe one of those ski patrolmen will help me. I snowplowed toward something called Climax.

4.

I am one horny fucking ski patrolman without a squeeze to call my own. Me and the boys work hard like pack mules and then we sit around all day and do nothing. It's like the Marines but without the war. We fight snow. The morning after a storm we load up the cannon and fire away.

Avalanche safety. Snow's not our enemy. We love it. We're on the same side, the side of weather, chaos, and the radical snowpack. Anyway, one day the summit shack was crammed with 10 of us and the subject of orgies came up. I stepped outside to get some air. I've participated in a few orgies in college and I didn't like them. What people don't realize is the person you most want in your mouth is always taken. Secondly, some pants shitter you'd never want within a mile of you is creeping up from behind, wanting a piece of you, and thirdly, it can get a little gamey when Joe Yuck sticks his gnarly arm pit or reeking foot in your face. Okay, so maybe I'm a little prissy, but I know what I want and I know who I am (I wear these 5 lb. lead hoop earrings that can take your eye out if we're dancing too rough). One day I was doodling away on my Patrolzine—a kind of private newsletter called *Sierra Serenade*, it has quite a following—and up walked Lars Stubenklonk. I go, Hey, are you circumcised? And he goes, Hell no, are you? I say, That's a big negative, Foreskin Brother, Christ prefers his flock uncut. We chortle together, and then I say, You want to pose for me tonight? Ten-four, Oil Can, see you . . . when? I say, Midnight, and you better be in leather. Fast forward to 11:45 P.M. I stuff my backpack with art supplies and a small bottle of sherry. We're climbing Huevos Grande, a bigass full moon lighting the way. When we reach the saddle I drop my pack and say, Hey Lars, pull out your cock, that's an order. He unzips and releases a killer slab. I bend him over a snowy boulder, plow his cinderblocks, and then the pig farmer returns the favor. Damn. Then we pack up our gear and continue our steep stroll. With Lars two steps ahead of me, I say, Fart in my face, you dumb ox. After a brief pause he releases the most profound intestinal horn recital my mind has ever translated into English. A fine aromatic concoction of meat, gasoline, and old socks. In a word, Yum. When we summit our favorite chute, I say, Bend over and show me your smelly crevasse, which he does, and I pound the cheese out of him, then I pull out my sumie brush and watercolors and paint for a while. I do a very loose rendering of my fist in his ice cave and then a sentimental sketch from memory of my old lace-up boots from childhood with the man in the moon in the background and then a snowman with a cock so big that it goes up to his nose. Then Lars and I click into our skis, do figure-8s down Huevos. He and I are going to Valdez for the championships. We're going to bring home that trophy and make America proud.

TECHNICALLY DADLESS

DEATH BY TOILET

A mother tells her son that murderers take great pleasure in hiding out near public restrooms, especially late at night, and that if he, her precious son, isn't careful he could end up six feet under, or worse. What's worse, Mom? Worse is when your body isn't recovered. You're in limbo. You're dead in theory, but technically you're still alive. Or maybe it's the other way around. I'm not sure, but you never get a funeral. And that's a shame. When a child disappears it is most troubling for the surviving family, the *loved ones*—in your case, your father and myself, and if you had a sister or a brother (thank God you don't), they would also experience undue emotional pain. The parents would be placed in a situation of *not knowing*. There's a technical term for that. I think it's called *hell in a crock pot* or *no closure for the little witch* or *grief dangles from faulty cables*. Needless to say, both your father and I would then be treated like suspects, and for good reason. No motive for killing is stronger than parent to child, with the exception of child to parent. It's often a contest. Who will strike first? Who will bury whom? People, which is another way of saying strangers (the blur of slime you see everywhere you go), and police (because it's their job), and friends (pseudo intimates; we all know how stretched and inaccurate that term is) with a sick sense of humor (because they like to torture those closest to them) will call us night and day, under the pretense of caring, *just checking in to make sure everyone is okay,* they will say, but in fact it's all a very sophisticated method of psychological torture. Mother, the boy asks, and, Shut up, let me finish, the mother continues, These people bring cold cuts and cakes to your house. They think you'll be hungry. But you're sick to your stomach with sorrow. Two seconds later these friends are ripping into the ham and roast beef. They're spreading mayonnaise on their earlobes. They'll say they're famished as fragments of meat shoot out of their mouth and whistle past your ears. Occasionally a chunk of ivory gristle lands on you. They apologize and then fire another piece of brown matter in your direction, secretly hating you for all the attention you're getting. They think you're milking the situation. The boy yawns. Cover your mouth when you do that, the mother says, and, don't use a public bathroom unless you go in with five or six friends—two should be on guard and vigilant, eyes constantly moving, on the lookout for suspicious men—or if there's an armed guard in front of the boys room, that's fine, but make sure he's authentic, check his badge, act like you come from an important family; there's a lot of fake law-enforcement types floating around who prey on children such as yourself. If my name comes up, refer to me as *Mother,* say it with a slight British accent if you can. Remember that game we used to play? I am a limey prig. Do that. Most sex offenders are intimidated by these sorts of things. You're our only son. We mustn't lose you. Not after all the money we've invested in you and all the love we've ladled out on your precious head. Other parents have two or three kids. Losing one isn't nearly as bad. They get over it. They dote on the others.

The siblings carry the bulk of the guilt like soldiers who witness the death of a close buddy—why them not me, a simple thought carried and turned over every day for their entire existence. If we lose you we'll go mad. I shouldn't speak for your father. I know I will. Now go to school.

In art class the boy puts the finishing touches on an animated movie he's shooting with a super-8 camera. He pulls white yarn through the stem of a pickle. Then he stands the pickle up and attaches the stem to the lower third of the pickle's body. Frame by frame the boy shoots the white yarn slowly creeping out of the stem. The teacher is pleased with the boy's innovation. Oh, that's semen, she says. A male pickle ejaculating onto a female pickle—that's not the safest or most reliable form of birth control. I had two abortions when I was in high school because I never used contraception. My boyfriends and I would use the pull-out method— which is no method at all, really, it's plain stupidity—but when I'm all hot down there sometimes I don't think and I'm just screaming for more. The guy would pull out at the last mega-second and cum on my belly, but inevitably a drop or two would make its way inside me, and since I'm the most fertile woman on the planet, it would always be straight to the pregnancy-termination center. The teacher says, I know the school bus passes that orgy house where all the Reef Girl models sunbathe naked. What a treat that must be. I hear all the boys jump out of their seats to get a better look. Makes going to school kind of a necessity. I know you're probably a little young for this, but next semester I'll bring in a book called the *Kama Sutra* which describes hundreds of positions a man and woman can be in when they have sex, each with a wonderful name like the Butterfly Plow and Circle K, all of which I have tried. The thing I learned was that different positions work for different body types. It's funny, when all is said and done, I'm really just an old-fashioned girl that likes the missionary position. I like being on the bottom. I like to look up and feel the weight of the guy. Also, I can really thrust back when I'm down there; it's like the crushed-petunia pose in yoga. If I'm on my side or on my hands and knees, it's sexy and everything, especially if we're in a motel and there are mirrors everywhere, but I'm not as agile as I'd like to be. You'll know what I'm talking about when you get a little older. And if you're gay and prefer being a bottom, well then, girlfriend, we're going to have plenty to talk about. The teacher gives a limp-wristed slap in the air. The boy writes *restroom assassin* in his notebook. Then he writes *don't flush*. Then he writes *wipe front to back, not back to front*. The teacher says, You can't have a movie without a movie poster. She hands out huge sheets of paper and charcoal. The boy draws pictures of knives, rows and rows of them, stacked up, single file, knives falling from the sky like snow. I love your knives, the teacher says. My first husband used to love to have sex with various accoutrements, including knives. He never cut me, thank heaven; I was just excited by the whole danger thing. These were in our cocaine and vodka gimlet days, before we got married. Once we exchanged rings and vows it was all downhill. Sad story. We both went into AA and straightened out our lives. Your knives are quite lyrical, the teacher says, focusing on the boy's drawing, but where are your two pickles? Your poster might mislead viewers, but only you have a clear vision of the final product. Why don't you draw hands? Hands and knives together. After the boy draws a picture of a hand stabbing another hand, the teacher leans over his desk and says, Now you're talking, try a face, to hell with the pickles. Soon the boy is drawing big heads with knives stuck into eye sockets and ears. The teacher sees a big curved line and suspects the beginnings of an ass. Ah, the butt crack, she says, we're not doing nudes until next week, but I'm not going to hold you back. The teacher drops the pencil she's holding and gazes at the ceiling, lost in thought. She smiles and says, The ass is a sacred area. It's the only place on the human body where tragedy and comedy reside together in conflicting harmony. Young man, you are a skilled draughtsman. The teacher walks to her desk and pulls out a tape recorder. She places it on the boy's desk. Then the school bell rings. Day over. Time to go home. I think you're ready to make sound art, she says. I want you to take advantage of all the interesting sounds on the way home. Don't take the bus. Walk. Put this microphone in unusual places.

On his way home, the boy walked through the park. He had to make a Number Two. The sun was going down. He saw a scruffy man in a bathrobe standing by the restrooms, holding a wire coat hanger. The boy pulled the tape recorder out of his backpack and pressed record. Hey mister, the boy said, are you going to strangle someone with that wire hanger? My mom warned me against people like you. He said, Let's go inside where no one will see us. He held open the door. After you, he said politely. I'm recording this for class, the boy said, do you mind if I ask you a few questions? That's cool, the man said, fire away. What's your favorite method of murder? He held up the coat hanger. Then he said, Actually, I prefer my bare hands. Why do you do it? Well, my father sort of did stuff like this and I'm just following in his footsteps. You got to follow your father. Strike that from the record; one can't help following one's father. You do everything you can to resist but there's something in the genes or the psyche that clings to the lineage no matter how destructive. But, aside from natural forces driving me to kill, it's just a great feeling, like riding a giant wave and surviving. It's a total rush. That sounds awesome, the boy said. Yeah, but it depends on who you kill; some people are not as enlightening as others are. For instance, I can't understand the appeal of killing the elderly. They're almost dead to begin with. There's no challenge there, plus they confuse you with their children. They think you're part of the family, one of their grandkids or nephews. You find yourself explaining who you're not right before they die, which is disconcerting. Plus, they're not challenging. They're physically so weak. They die at the drop of a hat. I tried to strangle one gentleman who offed himself with a heart attack the second I touched him. I like a little struggle. Also, old people tend to be religious, at least that's my experience. They babble. They'll say anything to survive. Why do you wear a bathrobe? Aren't you cold? No, I'm actually perspiring. I'm hot. I'm kind of nervous. This is my good luck bathrobe. It's never been washed. It makes me feel like I'm home in front of the TV no matter where I am. The boy said, That's enough questions for now. I have to go to the bathroom. The man said, Are you going to record it? You should. The whole kerplunk thing will sound great if you get your microphone close enough and then the big flushing sound. The toilet is the classic metaphor for a ruined life. The boy went into a stall. Leave the door open in case you need any help, the man said. I'll be fine, thanks, the boy said, and locked the door behind him, pulled down his pants, and sat on the toilet. The man in the bathrobe put the coat hanger down for a second and splashed cold water on his face. In the stall the boy spoke to the tape recorder. Here we are, ladies and gentlemen; I'm about to let loose a big nasty poop. We're hoping for a figure-8, but any configuration or letter of the alphabet will be considered kickass. It's only a matter of time. Wait, I feel something poking through; could it be, yes it is, the blind snake is venturing out of his hole. He's making an appearance. There he is. He's stretching farther and farther down. He's about to cut his losses and fall into the round sea. He's dangling quite nicely. Oh yes, he dropped right in. What a quiet little plop. Let's spin around and have a look-see. Ah, the letter U. Is the black butt-snake trying to tell me something? Should I leave the creature in the water for the next kid? So many questions. One thing is for sure, I must wipe, front to back, not back to front, like my mother taught me. The boy turned off the tape recorder and said, I didn't flush. The man with the coat hanger said, I know. I could hear every word. Maybe I'll tell the next kid that walks in here all about the kid who laid down the U-shaped turd. The boy said, Make him eat it.

When the boy returned home his mother was in the kitchen cooking. The boy said, Mom, I hate liver and onions more than anything in the world. The mother said, Wash your hands and set the table, your father should be home any second. The boy said, I'm doing so well in school that my teacher let me borrow a tape recorder. She told me to make sound art so I went to the park and met this really cool guy in a bathrobe that said he strangled little kids but he wasn't going to kill me for some reason. The mother said, You don't listen, do you? No matter what I say, it's in one ear and out the other. Before I had you I was an actress. I had a promising career in the theatre. I was in *Auntie Mame*, Off-Broadway. I wasn't much of a dancer, but I could sing. We were trained in those days. Not like now where the first thing the anorexia actress does is stuff her chest with silicon and pose naked. Now they're all prostitutes posing as thespians. I gave it all up to have you. I said goodbye to all that and I became one of the great mothers in the history of childbirth. I fed you with my own bosom. Now you tell me that whore teacher of yours gave you a tape recorder and told you to make sound art? The mother put down her wooden spoon and turned off the gas flame. The sizzling onions, which were once so loud, quit wiggling and grew quiet. The mother picked up a butcher knife and approached her son. No, Mom, the boy screamed. Yes, the mother said calmly. It is time. You've read the Bible. This happens now and again. It's the natural order of things. Plus, no son of mine is going to fornicate with his eighth grade teacher. I am not going to stand around and cheer while she licks and sucks on my baby. I will not light her marijuana cigarettes, nor will I provide her with a clean ashtray, nor will I change your disgusting sheets. I will not be ridiculed in my own house. You are a little bastard. Since when do you think it's okay to break every natural law known to man? The boy hit record and said, Mother attempting to kill her son, into the tape recorder. She took a swing at him with the giant blade, and the boy said, Tape recorder doubling as shield, son blocks deadly weapon, stabbing action continues. The boy dropped the machine. Batteries skidded across the linoleum. Liver and onions are my favorite, he said. I changed my mind. I love liver and onions. The mother lunged at him, knocking the phone off its cradle. The mother plunged the knife wildly, and repeatedly missed the flesh of her son. The boy picked up the phone and struck his mother on the head. She dropped the knife. She fell to the ground dazed. The boy wrapped the phone cord around his mother's throat in the same manner that a cowboy ties up the feet of a young calf. She struggled to breathe. The mother said, I have to set boundaries, a mother can't say yes to everything. At that precise moment, the father came home from work. He put his briefcase down and watched his son strangling his wife. That's interesting, he thought, before realizing the severity of the situation. He ran across the kitchen and jumped on the boy and slapped him across the face. Then he hugged and kissed him and started to cry. The boy cried. The father unwound the phone cord from around his wife's neck. Are you all right, he asked? I'm fine honey, she said. Mom tried to stab me, the boy said. The father said, Everyone wants to stab everyone, son. But that doesn't mean there isn't love in the air, flowers in our hands, and benevolence in our hearts.

CLIFF

My children disappoint the crap out of me. I haven't done anything wrong.

Cliff tried to teach his children to be normal. As toddlers they crawled across the carpet, sniffing furniture, licking up bugs and lint. When the children grew to teen-size, their behavior was no different; they refused to be human. A reasonable urge, or anti-urge—the limitations of being a person among people can seem, to the unenlightened citizen, an overrated pursuit. No argument there. His daughter said she wanted to be a butterfly, a hopeful declaration; and his son pretended he was a side of beef, or was it a vampire? Something having to do with veins, arteries, and pools of blood.

Like any perplexed father challenged by parenthood, marriage, and middle-life dilemmas, Cliff was going through some changes of his own. For instance, he didn't want to be heterosexual anymore. His petite, lemon meringue–flavored wife no longer ignited his oil spill. He wanted a foul-smelling male ogre to wreck his sorry ass, a wild boar that might rekindle long-buried passions.

Cliff's daughter confined herself to a caterpillar existence, lying around all day on the couch drawing pictures of wings. Not ready for butterflyhood. Maybe never. Hard to say. "I'm fine, really," she said, daily, to anyone who asked, "I love my daddy." She was only 15, with miles of life ahead of her. *My son, the boy is 17, hangs upside-down from a meat hook in his room that he has fashioned into a walk-in refrigerator, a brisk 42 degrees. He's emotionally distant, rigid, pale, currently registered in a low-residency vampire training program in Oregon that I'm paying for in quarterly installments. His incisors are sharpened, but lopsided.* The son had this to say: "Damage has been wrought. I am not whole, that is why I am a creature of the night."

Cliff made it clear to the world that he was the patriarch of the family, Chairman of the Board. He was financially liable, responsible for the family's every action. If either child used a weapon in a crime, the District Attorney would immediately look to the father. Cliff was to blame.

Question: What about the wife, his dessert-flavored spouse?

Answer: Like most women, she sought shelter, safety, intelligent conversation, and love, which is why she moved away to live with her mother.

Cliff's reaction: *The kids are saying the phrase, Right on, these days, so I'll say it, too . . . Right on.*

A bushy Eucalyptus tree, whose branches seemed to hold numerous birds and trash-diet vermin such as raccoons, opossums, and flying squirrels, spoke to him.

It was a windy day. Thick branches swayed in slow motion. The tree's message: "A policeman will pull you over for speeding. He'll try to rape you. Turn it into love." Several squirrels jerked their large tails and chirped out a mechanized sound that was secret code for approval. The wise, thoughtful tree, with so much integrity, had been stationed on earth far longer than Cliff.

Fast-forward to ecstasy. *Right now I'm very happy,* Cliff

announced, again, preferring to ride shotgun in this fiction and tell the tale himself rather than be inaccurately profiled. *I just had sex with a policeman in the backseat of his squad car, and I am under the impression that Officer Milk and I will see each other again. He asked for my phone number, said he'd call.* "No worries," was how he put it *(a figure of speech that induces mountains of anxiety in me, perhaps because I'm Jewish. You'd never hear Kafka say, "No worries").* Cliff fretted that he appeared grotesque and needy. He consoled himself with the thought that desperation is sometimes an appealing personality trait to the cold, waspy, all-American cop type who'd grown up on sports, violence, and meals featuring cloven-hoofed animals and lard.

And another thing: Don't assume the gentle handling, maneuvering, rotation of a nightstick is heinous until you've been on the receiving end of said black oak. After Officer Milk pulled Cliff over and asked if he knew how fast he'd been driving, he requested Cliff's driver's license, vehicle registration card, and proof of insurance. It was early morning. A small bird sat on a fence, staring at a field of cows, trying to select which thousand-pounder was best to land on and rest atop for the day. Officer Milk asked Cliff to step out of the vehicle. Cliff noticed the cop's rosy lips nestled behind a thicket of brown, porn-star moustache. *Hello, Fuller Brush man. Talk about cleaning up the neighborhood; that broom could sweep up Calcutta.*

When Officer Milk first brought the baton into their sexual conversation, Cliff thought, *Let's save the nightstick for jail and the last three minutes of my life* (he didn't actually think words). *I was gripped by horror in its purest form. I was frightened and nauseous. Then I thought, Just go with the flow, Mr. Rigidity, and believe it or not it was actually a perfect fit, you know, like when all the muscles in your legs and torso are totally relaxed . . . I just kept looking at the happy bird on the big cow . . . Plus, a nightstick is what, like three and a half fingers wide? No biggy.*

Cliff heard Officer Milk back there spitting in the general

direction of his bum, missing badly, wads of saliva, intended to be a natural lubricant, all over his backside, a gesture which gave this encounter a very contemporary feel since it was the new macho rage to spit at the orifice. With his eyes closed, he imagined a loud hippo or a water buffalo back there playing a loud juicy game. Being a naturalist or a humanist, it's hard to say which, and a regular consumer of pornography, Cliff was fond of guttural bile. Sometime during this 40-minute tryst, Cliff opened his eyes and noticed a large paisley-shaped leaf flutter through a backseat window. The leaf landed on the driver's-side headrest and murmured, "It's just another part of the human animal." The leaf was curved like a pale green smile. He pictured football players roughhousing on grass, spitting everywhere. *I am a gridiron.*

Yes, the ass is a 24-hour civil disturbance. "Fight crime," Cliff purred into the upholstery as the nightstick inched its way through him. Choking, too, when applied in small doses, has its place in lovemaking. It tells the partner in no uncertain terms that this exact moment is life or death. How come Officer Milk never choked him or cuffed him or burned him with his wonderful-smelling Dominican cigar?

This is all good to know, and useful in taking your mind off the aforementioned wayward children and separated wife.

I am a homosexual now. The transformation is complete. A member of the other church.

I spent the night in a motel and woke up disoriented but happy. I could feel it. The idea of love returning to my life, driven through me. I could feel it like a stake in my heart, or wherever, in my bottom-heart. I was actually bleeding.

Officer Milk never called like he promised.

When the children were young I had trouble sleeping. I used their beds with them in them. First one, then the other. There was a lullaby in my head. My intent was to hum, to make their sleep sound. To remind them how tight our family is.

Without warning, apropos of nothing, the children taught me things, contradicting my forecast of doom. For instance, I asked the daughter what the greatest artwork of the 20th century was and without hesitation she said the train. Her answer mesmerized me for days. My son, member of the undead, dreamer of jugular veins, sucker of human flesh, said he'd prefer being called Count. The name change suited him. He said that sunlight and garlic didn't bother him at all. When he was an infant, I used to call him Skipper. His big round head made me think of sailors.

There are days when no matter how fast or how badly you're driving a cop is nowhere to be found, and, if he does appear on the horizon, he isn't especially interested in your misconduct. Cliff had been driving erratically for a solid hour, on freeways and down main boulevards, in search of a hunky cop. When he finally spotted a black-and-white cruiser coming the other way, he waited until the two vehicles were very close before he hit the brakes and spun out. The two cops, who were both sporting fiery mirrored shades, drove by slowly, shook their heads in disbelief, and laughed. They passed a large messy burrito back and forth that they appeared to be sharing, taking giant bites and saying something that only made them laugh harder.

Wow, two hotties, and they won't pull me over?

Cliff was not their type, simple as that. Before the cops drove away, they tapped the horn twice, a little toot-toot, and the officer in the passenger seat leaned over the driver and gave Cliff a mocking demi-wave with his fingertips. Then at the last second, he tilted his head to the side and stuck out his tongue.

Fucking little flirting fucks. Think you're so tough with your badges and uniforms. I'll ram you with my rear end. How's that? You can make your inbred love in a hospital.

Cliff threw his car into reverse but the engine stalled. He took a deep breath and grabbed the steering wheel like it was a life preserver. He looked up and watched the cop car disappear down the street in his rearview.

Settle down there, little lunatic. I'm not hysterical. I think we're just trying too hard. Don't attack the policemen and wind up with bullet holes in your face. That's not our objective today.

Cliff, naked in the bathtub, an hour after the hot water has been turned clockwise (off), chin on chest, staring at his penis: *It's lost cartilage or tissue or whatever substantive things generate meaning, muscle, oomph. It really is just a pissing device at this point. Now I just inhabit the earth. There was a time when I used to really be here.*

OUR LIZARDS

My mother calls this morning to check up on me. The weekly call from Ann Arbor. I don't want to talk to her or anybody else. Why do I pay money to hear that little machine ring if all it does is wipe out my ever so fragile tranquility? Rarely do I use it to call out. Getting rid of the thing—it's my next big step toward becoming 100 percent unsociable. No phone. Reach me on the street. That's where I'll be.

It's been a bad week.

Whether I like it or not, my mother and I are talking away; there's nothing I can do about it. The same questions come from her, followed by my regular answers, my evasions. My life, no different than last week. All fucked up. I don't tell her this oh-so-terrible fact because she'll insist that everything will be fine. If I challenge her theory of the happy world, she cries. That's what I hate most. She feels responsible for the way I am, and I feel responsible for putting a kink in her smooth cheerful outlook. So I keep things from her. My mother gets upset when I tell her I'm sick of talking, or okay, that I'm in a quiet mood. That scares her. She thinks quiet is for the dead. She believes we should all think and say nice things as long as we're alive. And smile more. But Mom, I'm dying inside. I'm so incredibly unhappy.

No, can't say that. We hang up.

Ten minutes later, my older brother calls, obviously on orders from Mom. He doesn't know what to say.

"Lou, how are you?" he asks.

"Hey, I'm fine," I say, straining to sound upbeat. "How are you?"

He tells me about this trip he took to Florida. On the drive back, he stopped at a pet shop and purchased four lizards for his three children—four, just in case one died in the car. It would save him an explanation. All the lizards survived. Martin, the three-year-old, asked his daddy why there were four—who was the fourth one for? My brother told Martin that one of the lizards had a baby. Martin asked which one. My brother pointed at random. Martin asked where it came out, and my brother said underneath the tail.

Great. We hang up.

Unplug the phone.

My brother's approach to life is unsettling. I know he'll continue to tell his safe little lies forever. It'll never stop. But those common changes in the truth will turn him into a fake, and in 10 or 20 years his children won't even recognize him.

Who's the impostor? Where's Dad?

That's him. That's the guy.

I'm no different. We're both terrified of life.

When I used to think of dying, I always pictured myself stepping into the feeding ground of a tiger. The image just came to me one night and stuck for years. It seemed appropriate for who I was. I can't say why. Now I feel differently. I see another animal. I still want to be eaten alive; only now I would prefer a dip in the ocean followed by a serious attack from an angry sea lion. However unlikely that may seem, it's what I truly want. In the end I pray that I am torn apart. Not whole.

Maybe a walk would do me some good. Yes, a long walk. It's cloudy today. I'll put on my hat and fill up the canteen. Then I'll be off.

TECHNICALLY DADLESS

A dad briefly, five years, and then no dad. A dead mom, a sister I've never met, a little furry substitute for everything, Gluey, my pooch, named after my dad who's serving a life sentence in Leavenworth for living up to his nickname, by gluing people's mouths shut until they stopped breathing. As a little boy, I remember holding onto my dad's giant shoulders when he swam the breaststroke the length of a pool. The big hairy ride, my swimming bear. He made decent money as a carpenter, but he was paid 10 times that for performing unusual tasks for crooks he knew growing up in the neighborhood. His specialty was strapping a guy down onto his worktable and filling his mouth with glue. Then he'd flip them onto their sides and do the same to their ears. Speak no evil, hear no evil. If the guy was supposed to remain alive, he'd fill up their bung holes or seal up a man's genitals in resin the way a craftsman embalms scorpions in amber to make jewelry.

After my dad was taken away, I would like to say that I was raised by wolves, but I wasn't, unfortunately. I was brought up under the slow-moving gloom of my grandparents, Izzy and Ida. A cartoonist could zipper a blabbermouth's face shut and all the kids would laugh: My dad does it in real life and goes to jail forever.

I make drawings of people with webbed feet. I have dreams of becoming a frog. I'd like to remain a frog, sit half-submerged in a lagoon at 3 A.M. croaking with a gang of other frogs, eating insects, having sex with other slippery frogs. Never do I want to turn into a prince. I want to decapitate the prince.

My dad was a good father, a gangster in the grand tradition of Jewish gangsters, once a singular presence on the American scene, like the Jewish boxer or baseball player. I love him. He doesn't accept visitors anymore. Not even me. He'll draw a heart on a square of toilet paper and drop it in the toilet. He'll watch the ink bleed. Then he'll flush it down. I could see him doing that.

In the book *World of Dogs*, it says that Gluey, my furry partner with whom I prowl around, exudes a *shy mournful brilliance*. Truer words were never written. He smells the earth as if he were taking notes for an encyclopedia. A hummingbird jams its dipstick into a succulent flower, withdraws some juice, and flies away. I know it might seem disrespectful to name a dog after your own living father, a no-no in the Jewish religion, but I don't see it that way. My intention was to think of my dad whenever I shouted Gluey's name. I accept visitors. A woman so beautiful she causes trees to sway and bow when she walks by comes up to us, or to Gluey, and says, Hello, sweet thing. I could swear she says, Gallows geek spring, but that's not what she says, because she's talking to Gluey. She kneels down and both her knees make a faint cracking sound. She looks up and asks, What's his name? I say his name is Gluey. I kneel down with her and scratch his chest. The woman rubs his behind. Gluey's rear leg convulses. She says, Oh I got you now, what a sweet boy you are, Lou. She asks if he has any puppies, and you say he has puppies; would you like to come home with us and see all the puppies and pick your very favorite and take him or her home with you, would you like that? Oh yes, she says, that would be divine, fantastic; she follows us home, and while we're having sex, I have this vision that the inside of her body is lined with pink satin, then she whispers, while bobbing up and down on top of me, Open me up, so I say with the butcher knife, and she says, Yes, with that, so I reach for the huge blade that sits on the nightstand beside a stack of books and hack away only to realize that this beautiful girl is an ordinary human being with the same insides as everyone else and I didn't have to go and slice her up like that even if she begged me to do it; but I didn't. I just thought it up, so no harm done, none, no harm, still free to live and breathe. Gluey hangs his tongue out, drools a little thank you. He's tired maybe. The woman says goodbye and I tip my hat. I try to be polite to everyone.

MY TWO SONS

At first I was horrified when they drew swastikas on their foreheads, but then I remembered that all of their markers are water-based and non-toxic so there would be no side effects. I knew I could wash the swastikas off with soap and water, which I did as calmly as possible. I knew they'd kick and shriek. I anticipated that. No one likes his or her forehead scrubbed like a dinner plate. I also knew, and I still know—fathers are built for knowing—that a swastika doesn't necessarily connote bad things like Germany, human extermination and what's-his-name (A.H.), that it also stands for sex, energy, and rebirth in Native American cultures for example, and in Korea.

I'm going to lecture for a minute; this is what fathers do; it's in our job description. When we're not gathering logs, boulders, and berries, or hunting animal meat for dinner, we're called upon to spout wisdom.

Nothing prepares us for *the way we are*. Your brain sits on top of, or rather inside of, your head, commanding you to *do things* and you indiscriminately obey. You have no choice. *Go to the toilet*, the mind commands, *it is time.* And so you shuffle down the hall, turn a corner, and approach the chamber pot. Like a delivery truck, your buttocks are backed into position, pants and boxers dropped to the ankles. The next command is a simple, ominous, *descend.* Yes, Master, you silently say back to headquarters, as you bend your knees and drop your hindquarters onto the white plastic ring—a movement you complete like a hapless marionette. Does the contestant win a prize, you ask, since I pressed my ass cheeks onto the circle? No. He gets nothing. Instead he waits, and of course nothing happens in the bowel movement dept. No this and no that, which is another way of saying that we all have madmen at the control panels, steering blindfolded, giggling away, while all the buttons blink red and the knobs spin wildly. My ass cried wolf and my brains believed it. The hypothetical man didn't have to go potty, I said to Mr. Spider who crawled across the tile floor as flames engulfed the house in a nursery rhyme gone evil. Nothing was in there. It was a false alarm.

Something happened to me the day my kids were born. That's when the pilot—chained to the wheel with multiple padlocks (a brand name suspiciously called Master; it's all connected, my friend)—officially dozed off and never awoke. The pilot in me responds to things, but not very swiftly. At this stage of my life, I'd like to drill a hole in my head and drain out all the material. I retract that. I didn't mean what I just said. I'm happy. You can't raise kids unless you're cheerful. My smile is reinforced concrete with rebar jutting out from my upper lip.

Once my kids are in prison, they can get all the swastika tattoos they want. They can both be A.H. and destroy England together.

I get some pleasures. For instance, this morning I fell out of bed before the sun came up. While the water was boiling for coffee, I stepped outside to get the paper. I heard a funny sound. I shined a flashlight up in the tree and there was Alex, my son, 15 feet up, straddling a limb, nibbling on a pinecone. I said, Hey, what are you doing up there? Be careful. He worked furiously, making his way through the cone like it was corn on the cob. We stared at each other for several seconds. He wasn't *eating* the pinecone per se; he was just biting off pieces super fast and spitting out each little chunk to the ground, not unlike the action and method of a squirrel, which I think is his current role model. Alex can make that incredible clacking sound that squirrels make when they're threatened or horny. He's only seven.

I have a wife and two kids. I have other things as well like a pair of skis, a car, and a collection of peach pits. I am fond of peaches. I like to eat them, upwards of five a day. They're low-cal. A guy like me better watch his weight or he'll balloon into a circus animal. I especially love the peach pit's crenellated texture. Peach pits seem like miniature skulls. To be perfectly frank, nectarine pits separate a lot better from the fruit-meat than peach pits do. I'm not saying anything new here. Anyone who's consumed both types of fruit knows this. It's not important information for human survival, but it might tell you a little more about yours truly. I'm not sure what.

If I could be anyone else in the world right now, I guess I would choose to be a scientist. I'd experiment on animals and people. I'd like to make monsters. In my dreams I see frogs crossbred with pit bulls. But what am I talking about? My dream has partly come true. My wife (the professional sleeper) and I have two so-called *beautiful children*. I almost called them chickens. They're 100 percent people. I started to say chickens, maybe because when they were infants, I wanted to eat them; that's a normal adult reaction. The only difference for me was that when I held them close, and took a deep breath, all I could think was duck, turkey, chicken. When they acted up while we were barbecuing, I could see myself stripping them naked and slamming them down onto the hot grill, slathering them with Uncle Buster's Red Paste, and turning them into Tandori Brats. I could never picture my sons as ground beef (an unsavory thought). I'd cook and serve them country-style, full carcass. For some odd reason cannibalism has never bothered me, not even slightly. *Eat your own:* a motto I'd hammer above the hearth if I had the proper wood-burning tools and a little extra time for arts and crafts. But if truth be told, the only fellow who's going to get his head cut off around here is me—me chopping off my own. That's what razor-sharp knives and weights and pulleys are for. One beheads oneself when one's had it up to here. Don't think I don't think about this because I do, constantly.

When strangers tell my oldest boy that he has beautiful eyes, he kicks them in the shins. They're marbleized gray with streaks of blue. They look like precious stones. He's so handsome it's distracting.

When my sons grow up, I expect some part of the North American continent to be missing, just torn from the earth, stomped and burned, floating in the Pacific, drifting beyond Hawaii. I pray that they make it to 18, but I pity whoever is in their path. Right now the parents of underage criminals are being sued by surviving families. They're holding us responsible. They don't realize there's nothing we can do. The fierce monkey kills whenever it wants to. If you forbid the Catholic school girl with braids to run around with boys and lift up her plaid skirt, she will hightail it to the Wiggle Room and become a lady of the night. If you arm your children with weapons, they will join the Peace Corps. All I'm saying is being a parent ain't like it used to be. In one sense you could say it's more exciting. Girls, on the other hand, are less violent. That's a plus. But it would be insulting to say that girls are not capable of brilliant destruction. Unfortunately, I don't have any daughter to offend.

My wife is a very attractive smiling machine with the disposition of a cantaloupe—fragrant and watery. One of the boys is always screaming, cussing, throwing up; defecating in every conceivable room besides the john, in every possible receptacle besides the toilet. I privately refer to them as the two Charlie Mansons. They have actually written *pig* on the living room wall with their own excrement. They know that food is a weapon, also the sound of their voices, and the aforementioned deposits that the rear end manifests. Mix these things together and you have quite the juvenile arsenal. Then double it and make it so they are never held accountable. They both point at each other, *he did it, no he did it.* In the end, the villain is always me, the father, the tired blob who hasn't slept soundly since they were born, the chump who drained his bank account on their behalf. *Wait till we get to college,* they shout into a megaphone, or so I imagine, *we'll eviscerate your funds and encourage Mom to divorce you. We'll make up shit in court; you molested us when we were toddlers; you're currently sleeping with other women and lots of men; we'll Photoshop pictures of you doing nasty things to animals; we'll make you look fatter and even more unappealing than you already are so she'll think you're immoral and depraved cuz fat people always suck.* These are my own fears, my own neurotic babblements. None of it is true. Exaggerating my own problems makes me feel like everything's really okay, like maybe I have the perfect life.

"TORMENTING THE FATHER"
WRITTEN BY ME, THE FATHER
SPONTANEOUSLY PERFORMED BY THE WHOLE FAMILY

The following conversation takes place in our living room, a carpeted area 25 feet long, 15 wide. There are two hundred thousand toys scattered everywhere. Every step one takes, there's a good chance that a restful plastic creature will shriek itself to life and request affection or threaten you with violence. A person must be mentally sound when passing through this room. Once you hit linoleum, the room tapers into a very narrow kitchen, which is where I am, the father, when the curtain rises. I am 35 years old, going on 50. My two sons, Marco (five years old) and Alex (seven), are on the couch, on their backs, feet up in the air, their heads dangling off the seat like a couple of marsupials. They're very irritable. Before we begin, let me say this: It's easier for me to imagine my life in the form of a play. It's not as painful. But this is not a play. This is exactly what happened today, word for word. It's Home Life Vérité.

MARCO: Breakfast. Stop reading. Make us breakfast. Do it *nowww.*

ME: *(to the audience)* Marco's *now* lasts three seconds. He's stretched words out over a minute to emphasize a point. It's an effective method. I'll do anything to get him to stop. I was reading the newspaper. Back in the bedroom, my sleeping wife snores ever so faintly, not a speck of drool on the pillow. She insisted on getting pregnant two seconds after we got married. I am Commander in Chief of Saturday morning, or so I'd like to believe.

ME AGAIN: *(pretends to read the paper and then theatrically closes and folds it)* Good morning boys. *(standing at attention)* What would you like for breakfast?

ALEX: Cereal. *(sweeps an arm across the kitchen table, sending a pile of crayons and paper and a wooden Pinocchio to the ground)* Why do you always ask, Dad? You know what we want. The menu is a constant, like vomit and the solar system and vultures eviscerating dead cows.

ME: *(to the audience)* Alex's vocabulary is currently a runaway train. He's learning fast and it's scary. He loves all words that have to do with tearing apart bodies. A future Lee

Harvey Oswald or Jonas Salk? All I can do is spread love and hope for the best.

MARCO: Make us everything. Just make stuff. I'm ready to eviscerate.

ALEX: You used that word incorrectly, Marco.

MARCO: No I didn't, and so what if I did.

ME: Okay, we'll have a smorgasbord.

BOTH BOYS: *(look at each other, speak in unison, mildly disgusted)* Yeah, whatever.

ME: *(drops newspaper, walks into kitchen, ties an apron around waist)* You guys get a good night's sleep?

MARCO: We always sleep good. How come you always ask us that?

ALEX: Because he's a girl.

ME: I'll pretend I didn't hear that. *(grabs coffee, walks over to the refrigerator)*

MARCO: Like he's going to do anything.

ALEX: See me tremble.

MARCO: He likes wearing girl aprons.

ALEX: Hey, where's the remote?

ME: *(to the audience)* My kids are doing incredibly well in school. Their teachers love them and they get along great with the other kids.

ALEX: Dad, are you deaf? The remote. Find it. We're missing *Scooby-Doo*.

ME: Try looking between the cushions.

ALEX: No, YOU try looking in the cushions. YOU lost it.

ME: *(laying slabs of bacon onto skillet)* I'm in the kitchen. It's there somewhere. Who used it last?

MARCO: You did, lard man, now find it.

ME: *(chopping fruit)* I'm busy in here.

MARCO: Just come here now and find it. Find it, you insect.

ME: *(fussing with the bacon)* Hey, talk nice to your father.

ALEX: That's bullshit, Dad, find it.

ME: Alex, don't talk to me that way. You have to be nice or else I won't help you.

ALEX: All right, I'm nice now. See, I'm smiling. Now, find the remote. We're missing the beginning of *Scooby-Doo*.

MARCO: Hurry up, toilet fuck. Find the remote.

ALEX: He's such a jerk.

ME: *(laying bacon slices on a paper towel, pouring Cheerios into a bowl, adding milk)* Don't call me a toilet fuck.

MARCO: Okay, penis head.

The father is all smiles. That's right, I am, and I'm carrying a tray full of food into the TV area, placing it gently on the coffee table. Cheerios and milk for Marco. Cut up melon, pineapple, and peaches, and two strips of turkey bacon for Alex.

MARCO: Nope. Get it out of here. I told you before, no milk. I won't touch it.

ME: *(handing Alex his fruit and bacon)* Here you are, sir.

ALEX: On the table. *(pointing away)* Over there.

ME: What do you say? *(searching for sweetness and gratitude, a little manners)*

MARCO: Eat me raw.

ME: No. How do you thank someone?

ALEX: Shit man, get out of our face.

MARCO: Hey, *(screaming)* do you understand English, mister? Get these Cheerios out of here. No milk.

ME: *(to the audience)* I used to wash their mouths out with soap but I was worried I might poison them because they were cursing me all day long and the trips to the bathroom turned into hourly events. It started to get out of control. I'd be in the supermarket looking at mild punishment soap rather than soap for hands and body. But they taunt me.

ALEX: Give us some soap. Come on, Mister Big, try it, see if we care.

MARCO: Soap soap soap.

ALEX: You think you're so tough with the soap. We like the taste, okay, boy?

MARCO: Ivory, Camay, doesn't matter to us. Bring it on.

ALEX: Yeah, I like Lava.

ME: *(to audience)* Today is Marco's birthday. I always get two presents so whoever's birthday it isn't doesn't get angry and jealous and cry all day and break things and refuse to eat. I got Marco a battery-operated tyrannosaurus rex with moving appendages and growling voice. There's a handle on the big lizard's back with a trigger so you can move all the body parts and make him roar. Non-birthday Alex gets some kind of ball with two rackets. For a short time, the T-Rex is a hit. Then something imperceptible happens.

MARCO: *(angry)* Hey, this present sucks. It's dumb. I don't want it.

ALEX: Give it to me then. Let someone less fortunate than you have a chance.

MARCO: *(slamming T-Rex to the carpet, speaking to Alex)* Here. You can have it. This present sucks royal.

ME: *(crestfallen)* Careful. You could break it.

ALEX: You're right, it does suck.

MARCO: You promised me we'd go fishing. Let's go, now. I command you.

CURTAIN

SCENE 2

The curtain opens to reveal the father and two boys standing on a bridge, fishing. The mother/wife is 10 feet away, reading a magazine, dangling her feet off the edge of the bridge. A beautiful waterfall in the background.

ME: *(to the audience)* Since the kids were born, my wife and I have only had sex in hotels. Never once in the house. Anyway, I buy three rods and reels and some lime-green bait out of a jar. We drive to Convict Lake where a hundred years earlier, actual criminals drowned in a shoot-out with the law. I spend two hours untangling the kid's lines, first one then the other. I never once sip a beer. I don't even remove it from the ice chest. There's no time to light my cigar. I haven't even turned around to look at the waterfall. It's like I work in an untangling factory. At one point both fishing rods need work.

ALEX: Dad, you're taking too long. What's wrong with you?

MARCO: He's a diaper.

The father accidentally kicks one of the boy's fishing poles into the water. It quickly sinks.

ALEX: *(irate)* You cocksucker. You are a total jerk. Why did you do that?

ME: *(sheepish)* It was an accident, son. I'm sorry. Give me a break.

MARCO: No breaks for idiots.

ALEX: You better buy me another one. You owe me. *(face contorting)* You are so stupid.

ME: Don't talk to me like that, son. Talk nice, I'm your father.

ALEX: Just buy another fishing line and then you'll be my father. Just buy it and shut up. And quit trying to act like you're the boss cuz you're not.

MOTHER: Honey, I'm going to the store for a sandwich.

ME: There are lots of nice things in the cooler that I prepared.

MOTHER: You know I don't like mayonnaise.

ALEX: Mom, why are you married to Dad? He's so retarded.

MARCO: Yeah, Mom, you're cool. We're going to the store with you. *(the three of them walk away)*

CURTAIN

"It would be useless to expect to hear heaven murmuring in your windows. Nothing, neither your appearance nor the air, separates you from us; but some childishness more profound than experience compels us to slash away endlessly and to drive away your face, and even the attachments of your life."
—Antonin Artaud, Letter to the Clairvoyant, 1927

How badly I want to say that my kids love me and we have a great relationship. I can say it, fool myself into hoping that something will change. It's just that we've gotten a bad start. Most mornings I get up early and hang out in the cellar. For the record, I illustrate children's books. I draw all day long. I can't put the pen down. I love to draw more than talking, eating, or sexual intercourse with my spousal team member. When my wife hears the boys talk in an abusive manner, she asks them to stop, but it's never heartfelt and they know it. They know she appreciates their verbal assaults. They're speaking for her. The kids need to be creative, she might say, if she ever spoke.

ALEX: *(to the reader)* This play I'm in isn't over until I say it's over and it ain't, so open up the stupid ugly curtain *nowwwwwwwwwwwwwwwwwwwwwwwwwwwwwww.*

The curtain rises. Little three-foot Alex is sitting on a large stool.

ALEX: *(to the audience)* Thank you. I was named after Alexander the Great, and like him I have a great passion for Homer. I will not kill my father, Steve, for the same reason that my namesake from 338 B.C. didn't kill his, though he was suspected of it. Like he, I have more important matters to attend to, and if you think a seven-year-old doesn't sound like this you are an even bigger pile of shit than my dad is. If I were a dad I'd take my kids and string them up with rope, upside-down, and leave them there till they were old enough to bring home money. Only then would I cut them loose.

MARCO: *(approaches stage left; carrying a stool with both hands, he climbs onto the seat and addresses the audience)* I'm younger and smaller than my brother and I can kick his ass. I walk up to him and smash him in the face with a pillow any day of the week and he cries. I like guns. I want a gun. I like decapitations. Heads look cool rolling on the floor. I'd like to cut off my dad's head but if I do that he'll probably stop buying me presents so that wouldn't be smart. Keep the presents coming, keep the head from rolling down the street, that's what it's all about. The hardest thing for me is the distance between birthdays and Christmas. Big long gaps, all saggy and worthless. I could kill my dad and no one would care. My mom would sit with me at the defense table like a crybaby and my punishment would be next to nothing. I'd still get presents on my birthday and Christmas, and that is so much the only thing that matters.

ALEX: *(to the audience)* Since our mom's a pretty lady, we'd get a new dad real fast. She'd just sit around at the zoo and flirt, swish her bottom in front of the elephant keeper or the lion tamer, or she'd come to our school and play doctor with our principal, Mr. White, and that would be the new dad and hopefully he'd be more fun to play with than our original idiot. From what little I know of the world, our second dad will beat us up a lot. Stepdads like to beat up on the lady's kids because we get in the way of their going all the way. We distract our mom with bad grades, and we need a constant flow of money, and because we wish our first father would return. Maybe that's what will happen. We don't know how good we had it. Okay, original stupid, retarded, Steve-Dad. Don't die. Don't go away. Stay with us. We wuv you. I think it would be best if we let him finish the story. I'm ready for bed and everything he says is boring which leads directly to sleep. Dreaming of killing him isn't a crime. I want to see his head fly off in slo-mo. And then play it back at regular speed and see it reattach. I saw that in *Blood Gore 3*, the coolest CD-ROM in existence.

It's bedtime. The boys are tucked neatly under the covers and kissed on their foreheads. I hear them talking. They express their rough love in subtle ways. I jump into bed first, excited at the thought that I will soon be unconscious. I take a few hits of marijuana to obliterate my dreams. It's not fair to make me dream. I sleep in my boxers and the T-shirt I wear underneath my day clothes. I have pajamas, but I only wear them when I'm sick. I dangle one bare foot off the side of the bed so I never overheat. My wife thinks that's cute. I'm grateful that I can do something that generates a response like that. She goes so far as to say that my barefoot cooling system is *sexy*. My wife takes her clothes off in front of me. She has the stripping skills of an exotic dancer. She takes her bra off like Houdini slipping out of a straitjacket. I still can't figure it out. She steps out of her pants and folds them neatly over my gentleman's helper that my dad passed on to me. After snuggling up next to me, she says she'd like to have another child, a girl, and she'd like to start trying tonight. She sticks a finger in her mouth and touches me on my forearm. She's such a pro. I love you, she says, reading cue cards from hell. I love you too, I say back.

In 20 seconds something incredible happens and we haven't checked into a hotel. Later, I'm in basic *Kama Sutra* position 1-B and her eyes are closed. Her breathing increases, she looks at me. Eye contact is rare for us. With a free hand I wave, like I'm across the street. That's a suave move. She smiles. She doesn't mind that I'm an idiot. I have sperm. That's all that matters. I'm not cynical; I'm a human resource. We switch to position 2-A and the countdown begins.

After liftoff, I sigh, she sighs.

I love the name Hope, she says.

Yeah, that's nice, I say. What do you think of Joy?

Other selections in Dennis Cooper's LITTLE HOUSE ON THE BOWERY series

VICTIMS by Travis Jeppesen

189 pages, a trade paperback original, $13.95, ISBN: 1-888451-42-4

"This book marks the debut of an author who will surely become a major voice in alternative literary fiction . . . rich, lyrical language reminiscent of a modern-day Faulkner informed by the postmodern narrative strategies of Dennis Cooper."

—*Library Journal* (starred review)

HIGH LIFE by Matthew Stokoe

326 pages, a trade paperback original, $16.95, ISBN: 1-888451-32-7

"Stokoe's in-your-face prose and raw, unnerving scenes give way to a skillfully plotted tale that will keep readers glued to the page . . . Stokoe's protagonist is as gritty and brutal as they come, which will frighten away the chaste crowd, but the author's target Bret Easton Ellis audience could turn this one into a word-of-mouth success."

—*Publishers Weekly*

GRAG BAG by Derek McCormack [forthcoming, June 2004]

203 pages, a trade paperback original, $14.95, ISBN: 1-888451-59-9

"*Grab Bag* culls the best of the perverse and innocent world of Derek McCormack. The mystery of objects, the lyricism of neglected lives, the menace and nostalgia of the past—these are all ingredients in this weird and beautiful parallel universe."

—Edmund White

Also available from Akashic Books

SOME OF THE PARTS by T Cooper
Selected for the Barnes & Noble Discover Great New Writers Program
264 pages, trade paperback, $14.95, ISBN: 1-888451-36-X

"Sweet and sad and funny, with more mirrors of recognition than a carnival funhouse, *Some of the Parts* is a wholly original love story for our wholly original age."

—Justin Cronin, author of *Mary and O'Neil*
(2002 PEN/Hemingway Award Winner)

ADIOS MUCHACHOS by Daniel Chavarría
Winner of a 2001 Edgar Award
245 pages, paperback, $13.95, ISBN: 1-888451-16-5

"Daniel Chavarría has long been recognized as one of Latin America's finest writers. Now he again proves why . . . [L]ed by Alicia, the loveliest bicycle whore in all Havana."

—Edgar Award-winning author William Heffernan

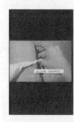

SUICIDE CASANOVA by Arthur Nersesian
370 pages, hardcover binding into hard-plastic videocassette, $25.00, ISBN: 1-888451-30-0

"Sick, depraved, and heartbreaking—in other words, a great read, a great book. *Suicide Casanova* is erotic noir and Nersesian's hard-boiled prose comes at you like a jailhouse confession."

—Jonathan Ames, author of *The Extra Man*

These books are available at local bookstores.
They can also be purchased with a credit card online through www.akashicbooks.com.
To order by mail send a check or money order to:

AKASHIC BOOKS
PO Box 1456, New York, NY 10009
www.akashicbooks.com, Akashic7@aol.com

(Prices include shipping. Outside the U.S., add $8 to each book ordered.)

Benjamin Weissman is the author of *Dear Dead Person* (High Risk Books/Serpent's Tail, 1995). He has written for various art and ski magazines, including *Artforum*, *Freeze*, *Frieze*, *Parkett*, and *Powder*. Weissman is also a visual artist whose work has been shown in the U.S. and Europe. He is represented by Galerie Krinzinger in Vienna. A professor at Art Center College of Design and Otis College of Art, Weissman lives in Los Angeles.